NANCY DREW MYSTERY STORIES

THE MYSTERY OF THE
BRASS BOUND TRUNK

BY

CAROLYN KEENE

Brenda Tuleya
4205 Beluven Pr.
Greensboro, N.C.

ILLUSTRATED BY

RUSSELL H. TANDY

NEW YORK

GROSSET & DUNLAP

PUBLISHERS

Made in the United States of America

CONTENTS

"TWO MEN ARE TRYING TO STEAL TRELDY'S TRUNK!"
NANCY WHISPERED.

The Mystery of the Brass Bound Trunk

CHAPTER I

A VALUABLE GIFT

NANCY DREW swung her tennis racket into a corner of the front hall.

"Any news since I went to the courts?" she asked the housekeeper, Hannah Gruen, who came through the doorway at the moment to greet the slender, golden-haired girl.

"Someone telephoned while you were gone. A woman; a very unpleasant person, I must say!"

"Did she give her name?"

"No, she refused, although I asked her twice. She made me understand she would talk only with you. I thought she seemed angry about something."

"I can't imagine who it could be," Nancy said, frowning thoughtfully. "I haven't offended anyone to my knowledge. Oh, well, she'll probably call later."

"I'm certainly glad you're home," said Hannah with a sigh, "because I've been worrying

1

about your trip to South America. You'll never be ready in time to sail. It's a mystery to me how you ever expect to have a trunk full of attractive clothes like the other girls if you don't even think about them!"

Nancy laughed, not in the least disturbed by the friendly scolding.

"Oh, it will be days before my boat sails, Hannah. It's more important to see that Dad gets started on his trip West. I'm worried about that. He's so serious and mysterious about this latest law case of his. I hope it won't be a dangerous one."

For several moments Nancy stared thoughtfully from the window, then added, "Good old Dad. Well, after he leaves I'll just toss a few things into a trunk and take off for South America as lightly as a bird."

"I wish it were as easy as that," Mrs. Gruen replied, sighing. "We haven't any suitable trunk. You need a strong one for traveling."

"I do need a new trunk," the girl agreed, her attractive face clouding.

"And you'll have to do a lot of other shopping," advised the housekeeper. "Remember, you'll be with those girls from Laurel Hall School."

"I'm not worried, Hannah. My chums George and Bess and I should be able to hold our own with them!"

"I wonder if the Senora who is headmistress will let George be called George," laughed the housekeeper. "She may not approve of a girl who has a boy's name!"

Nancy wrinkled her nose and smiled, a habit which often won her points in arguments. "We'll see," she said.

The attractive girl was the only child of Carson Drew, a well-to-do lawyer and widower, who resided in River Heights. Endowed with a good figure, a clear complexion, intelligent blue eyes and a pretty face, she never concerned herself deeply with her appearance. Yet in truth she was excited over the prospect of new clothes and a trip.

Nancy knew that she owed the coming voyage entirely to the fact that her father's business affairs required his presence in the West. Unwilling to leave his daughter alone during his absence from River Heights, Mr. Drew had arranged for her to travel to South America with a group of girls from Laurel Hall. Bess Marvin and George Fayne, who were Nancy's dearest friends, had persuaded their parents to allow them to accompany her, so the three were looking forward to a pleasant vacation.

"I have such a lot of work ahead," Mrs. Gruen murmured. "Your father's clothes must be packed because he hasn't time to do it himself. Then the house has to be cleaned and closed."

"I'll help you, Hannah," Nancy promised quickly. "We can work fast, once we start. As soon as I change my clothes we'll begin."

She took a shower, put on fresh clothing, and was combing her hair when the front doorbell rang. Mrs. Gruen opened the door. For a few seconds she stared at an object on the porch, then uttered a startled cry.

"Goodness me, what is this?"

As Nancy hastened downstairs, the woman picked up a large covered basket and started to unfasten the lid.

"Someone left this on our doorstep," the housekeeper said, her voice trembling with excitement. "Oh, I'm afraid—I just know it's an abandoned baby!"

Nancy took the container and raised the lid. Then she laughed. Curled inside was a large Angora cat, a blue silk ribbon tied about its neck.

"Well, of all things!" exclaimed the astonished woman. "A cat!"

"Isn't it a darling?" Gently Nancy lifted the pet from its silk cushion. "I wonder who left it here?"

Quickly she glanced up and down the street. No one was in sight, but a black automobile was rounding a corner.

"I think the basket was left by someone in that car, Nancy. Of all the tricks! What are we to do with a cat?"

"You don't look very pleased," chuckled the girl, stroking the animal's soft fur. "Here is a tag attached to the ribbon. Maybe it will explain everything."

She untied the string, then read the card aloud:

" 'To Nancy Drew, in gratitude for her help in the past.' "

"Who signed it?" inquired the housekeeper, peering over the girl's shoulder.

"No name is attached. It just says 'A Friend.' "

"I guess that's why the machine drove away so fast. The person didn't care to be seen."

"I can't figure out who would give me a cat, Hannah."

"Someone you helped. But then you've helped so many persons. What in the world will you do with it?" the housekeeper asked pointedly.

"Keep it, of course. You can tell that the cat is pedigreed and valuable. I think I'll call her Snowball. That would just about suit her, for she's so white and soft looking."

"You haven't by any chance forgotten you're sailing for South America in a few days?"

"Perhaps you could look after the kitten while I am away——"

"Oh, no," interrupted Mrs. Gruen. "I never cared much for cats, and I'll not saddle myself with such a responsibility during my vacation."

"Then I'll take Snowball with me!"

"All the way to Buenos Aires?"

"Why not? Snowball would love to travel, I know."

"A nice time you'll have, looking after a

cat!'' the woman protested. "But then, if you want to burden yourself, I guess no one can keep you from it."

Nancy laughed. With the kitten cuddled on her shoulder she started into the house, but paused as she saw a large delivery van turn into the driveway.

"Did you order something from the store?" she questioned Mrs. Gruen.

"Why no, I didn't. It must be a mistake."

Two men came up the walk bearing a good looking steamer trunk decorated with brass bindings and an ornamental lock.

"Shall we leave it here, or take it inside?" one of the deliverymen inquired.

"There must be a mistake," Nancy remarked. "I'm afraid you have the wrong house."

"This is the Drew residence, isn't it?"

"Yes."

"Then we have the right place. This trunk has been marked and can't be returned."

On the front the man indicated two initials, N. D., made in brass to match the other trimmings.

"That stands for my name," Nancy said in awe. "This trunk must be meant for me. Do you suppose Dad bought it?"

As if in direct answer to her question, a car rolled into the driveway. Carson Drew, tall and dignified, walked to the porch.

"I see the trunk is here," he observed, stooping to examine it. "Do you like it, Nancy?"

"Oh, it's perfectly beautiful, Dad. Did you really buy it for me?"

"Of course. Hannah told me you needed one. I had your initials put on it so you'll have an easier time identifying your luggage on the boat. I trust it fits your needs."

"Oh, it certainly will, Dad. Thank you so much."

"There must be a lot of folks traveling," said the expressman as he moved off, pocketing a nice tip from Mr. Drew. "I wish I was goin' somewhere myself."

"I wish you were," said Nancy kindly, as she directed the men where to set the gift in her room.

"Like as not Nancy will come back with her new trunk full of mysteries!" laughed Mrs. Gruen to the girl's father.

"Don't even whisper that word in my daughter's presence," said the lawyer, pretending to be stern. "I'm hoping she'll have a very quiet trip with no unusual adventures."

"Oh, Dad," Nancy said in quick protest, as she heard this last remark, "I can't imagine a vacation without a mystery to solve!"

"Speaking of mysteries reminds me that you could do something for me while you're on your trip," replied her father.

"Good. What is it?"

Mr. Drew glanced at his watch. "I haven't

time to tell you now," he said. "I just ran over here for a minute to make certain the baggage was delivered."

"Oh, Dad, it isn't fair to give me a little hint and then not tell me any more!"

"Come to my office if you have time," the lawyer flung over his shoulder as he walked to his car. "I'll give you all the details there."

After Mr. Drew had gone, Nancy and Mrs. Gruen admired the brass bound trunk anew. They also gave the cat a saucer of milk and were delighted with the animal's friendliness.

"Please look after Snowball while I'm gone," Nancy said to the housekeeper. "I must run downtown and talk with Dad."

The girl backed her own car from the garage and started toward her father's law office in the business section of River Heights. Enroute she paused at Bess Marvin's home to report the two splendid gifts, then sped on.

A traffic light flashed red. Automatically Nancy stopped. Scarcely had the wheels come to a standstill when her car was struck hard from behind. There was a loud crash, a crumpling of metal, and the girl was thrown violently against the steering wheel.

CHAPTER II

RECOVERING from the stunning blow she had received, Nancy sprang from her car. One glance disclosed that a gray coupe, approaching the intersection at high speed, had failed to stop at the red light. Its driver had attempted to swerve his machine aside, but it had struck and crushed the rear right fender of the Drew car.

"Oh, see what you've done!" Nancy cried in dismay.

The man in the other machine, a young fellow of perhaps twenty-two, with red hair and a tiny brush of a mustache, sat gripping the steering wheel. He took a handkerchief from his pocket and nervously wiped his forehead.

"I am sorry," he apologizd in a high-pitched voice. "I didn't see the light change until it was too late to stop."

As Nancy inspected the damage she said, "You must have been disobeying the speed laws or you never would have crashed into me so hard."

"I might have been going a little too fast," admitted the young man. "But please, I beg

9

of you, don't report the accident to the police."

"Of course you'll pay for all this damage!" said Nancy. "My car will need another fender and probably a lot of work done on it."

"Take this!" suddenly cried the other driver, shoving a bill into her hand. "It should cover everything."

Before Nancy could say a word, he backed up his car, gave the steering wheel a whirl, and shot down the street.

"Well, of all the nerve, to run off like that!" the girl exclaimed indignantly. "I'll get his license number!"

Before the auto was lost around a bend in the road, Nancy made certain of the numbers. After writing them down on the back of an old envelope she glanced at the money in her hand. To her surprise she saw that she was holding a hundred-dollar bill.

"He paid me generously enough," she thought, somewhat mollified. "I doubt that it will cost this much to get the car repaired."

While it was clear to Nancy that the young man must be a person of considerable means, she was puzzled by his actions. Why, she wondered, had he feared to have the accident reported?

By nature Nancy had an inquiring mind, and it was this faculty which more than once had drawn her into adventure and intrigue. Years earlier she had aided her father in solving a mystery case, familiarly known to her friends as "The Secret of the Old Clock." Since then he had often assigned special sleuthing work to her. Many other persons sought her aid in handling problems of mystery, so the girl had gained an enviable reputation as an amateur detective.

Her latest exploits, told in "The Clue of the Tapping Heels," concerned an unfortunate lad whose cruel guardian sought to profit at his expense. In bringing the man to justice, Nancy and her chums also met and aided an elderly actress who had suffered a reverse of fortune. They assisted in presenting a remarkable stage show and devised their own tap dance routine which could be executed in code. This same dance served a more vital purpose than entertainment, when the girls found themselves confronted with a situation which demanded quick thinking and courage.

Nancy's thoughts were far removed from mystery as she ruefully inspected the damaged car. The rear fender had been jammed so hard against the tire that she feared a tow-truck would be required to haul the wreck to the nearest garage.

"Hello," suddenly called a voice from the sidewalk. "What have you done now?"

Glancing up, the girl saw her friend, Ned Nickerson coming toward her.

"What have *I* done?" Nancy echoed with an

indignant wail. "Did you see what happened? This accident wasn't my fault. A man just ran into my car and then drove away as fast as he could!"

"He certainly made a nice mess of your machine," Ned said, shaking his head. "You'll never get a penny, either."

"Oh, won't I? Just look at this!"

Ned whistled softly as he saw the hundred-dollar bill. "Maybe it's counterfeit."

"If it isn't genuine then I'll trace down the man and send him to jail! I took his license number before he got away. Do you think I can get the car fixed for a hundred dollars?"

Ned gave her an amused glance. "Say, you ought to be able to rebuild it for that! Here, give me a hammer and I'll straighten out the fender so the wheel will turn."

He dived for the tools in the rear compartment. Soon he had hammered the bent metal into a semblance of its former shape.

"I know a reliable garage down the street a block," the boy told her. "Jones Brothers."

"Will you ride along with me?" Nancy pleaded. "You know just what needs to be done and I don't."

"Maybe I could help some," the young man acknowledged, pleased at the compliment. "Sure, I'll be glad to go along."

The car bumped slowly down the street, attracting considerable attention from pedestrians. Nancy turned into the garage and waited anxiously while Ned and the mechanic discussed the extent of the damage.

"The axle isn't bent so that's good news," presently young Nickerson reported. "He wanted seventy-five dollars to put the car in first class condition, but I convinced him the job was worth only fifty."

"Oh, thank you, Ned."

"That leaves a nice profit of fifty dollars for yourself. Not bad."

"The money isn't really mine," Nancy protested quickly. "I'll have to give it back to that young man."

"How will you ever find him?"

"I'll trace the license number," Nancy said quickly. "But I'll not have much time before my boat sails. How long before I'll have my automobile again?" she inquired of the mechanic, gathering up her purse and gloves from the seat.

"Not until tomorrow night."

"Oh dear," the girl sighed. "I'll need it for so many errands."

"I'll be glad to let you use my old bus," Ned offered generously. "Will you need it now?"

"No, I was on my way to Dad's office. That's only around the corner. Thanks for the offer and all your help."

Saying good-bye, Nancy walked a block to the tall building where her father had his offices. As he was busy with a client she waited ten minutes before being able to see him alone.

"You didn't waste much time in coming," he smiled in greeting a few moments later. "Unfortunately you've arrived at an awkward moment. I am due for an important conference in five minutes."

"Oh, Dad, after all the trouble I have had in getting here!"

"I'll tell you as much as I can about the case I want you to work on," Carson Drew said hastily. "It concerns an old client of mine, a man named Trenton."

"Do I know him, Dad?"

"I think not. He has a daughter named Doris, a rather charming girl, I understand."

"Is she about my age?"

"No, Doris must be older, around twenty or twenty-two, I'd say. Mr. Trenton tells me that she was formerly a very docile young woman, willing to listen to the suggestions of her parents."

"You say formerly?"

"Yes; but of late the girl has become unmanageable. Mr. Trenton has begun to lose patience with her."

"In just what way is the girl unmanageable, Dad? After all, she's twenty-two."

"For one thing, she refuses to marry a certain young man favored by her father. His name is Henry Washburn. He's the son of Mr. Trenton's deceased partner. The match would be an excellent one."

"From Mr. Trenton's standpoint or from Doris's?" Nancy inquired dryly.

"Well, I rather think myself that the question of money may be involved," Mr. Drew declared. "Trenton is reputed to be a wealthy man, but I know he lost a large amount last year. The marriage undoubtedly would not be detrimental to his business interests."

"If the girl doesn't love Henry Washburn I shouldn't blame her for becoming unmanageable! Her parents should be more reasonable," Nancy declared.

"Mr. Trenton is an old client of mine," Mr. Drew said with a smile. "That is why I promised to do what I could."

"I don't see what this case has to do with me," said Nancy.

"I'll tell you," replied her father. "Mr. Trenton has reached the point where he threatens to disinherit Doris unless she obeys his wishes. Now, as she is sailing——"

Nancy was destined to learn no more, for at that moment a secretary came into the room to say Mr. Drew's client had arrived.

"We'll talk further about this later," the lawyer said, dismissing his daughter with a wave of the hand. "Tell Hannah I may be late to dinner."

Nancy walked home slowly, thinking over what her father had told her. He had been so busy that she had not even had an opportunity to mention the automobile accident; but that news would keep.

Drawing near her home, Nancy was somewhat surprised to notice a chauffeur-driven car standing in front of the door. She stared curiously at it as she walked around the house, wondering to whom it might belong. Scarcely had the girl entered the kitchen when Hannah Gruen came hurrying from the living room to speak to her.

"Nancy, that woman is in there waiting for you!" she whispered.

"What woman?"

"Why, the one I was telling you about. She telephoned earlier this afternoon and when she came a while ago, she said she'd stay here until you got back."

Slowly Nancy removed her hat and gloves.

"I'll talk with her in just a moment, Hannah."

"I wouldn't if I were you," the housekeeper warned the girl soberly. "I can tell she's provoked about something you've done. If I were you, I'd slip out the back way and not return until she has gone!"

CHAPTER III

An Unpleasant Visitor

"Oh, I shouldn't think of running away," Nancy replied, rather amused at the housekeeper's suggestion. "I've done nothing to be ashamed of."

"But this woman is mean despite her fine manners," whispered Mrs. Gruen. "She has such a hard spoken way about her."

"Did she give her name?"

"Mrs. Thomas Joslin."

"I don't recall hearing it before," Nancy said thoughtfully. "Well, I'll see her. She may have mistaken me for some other person."

The visitor, who had advanced well into middle age, wore a tight fitting suit with an expensive fox fur thrown over her shoulders. Beneath a nose-length veil her sharp brown eyes studied the girl with undisguised scorn.

"So you are Nancy Drew?" she asked quickly.

"Yes, Mrs. Gruen said you wish to see me."

"Indeed I do. I have considerable to say. I'll not mince matters," the woman said coldly. "I have come here because I understand you expect to take a trip with a group of Laurel Hall girls.''

''Yes, that is true.''

''Then you will be compelled to change your plans!''

Nancy wondered if she had heard the woman correctly. As Mrs. Joslin waited for her to reply, she said easily, ''Will you explain why I should change them?''

''Because I'll not have my daughter Nestrelda associating with any girl who goes around prying into people's affairs, that is why!'' the woman exclaimed. ''I am sure I don't know why you were ever asked to join the group in the first place. It was a mistake on the part of the headmistress to include a—a detective with the others.''

With difficulty Nancy kept control of her temper.

''I suppose you are saying these things because you have heard I happen to have solved a few mysteries. I am not a professional detective in any sense of the word.''

''Nestrelda has been brought up to mingle only with persons of her own set,'' said the woman haughtily.

''I am certain, Mrs. Joslin, that you are under a wrong impression. You don't know me. Would you mind telling me just what you do mean?''

''I'll not elaborate,'' the woman retorted. ''I will grant that you look like a nice girl and you speak very well, but looks are deceiving!"

"Yes, they can be," agreed Nancy.

Mrs. Joslin stared hard at the Drew girl, then said, "My daughter is beautiful."

"I suppose so," murmured Nancy.

"She is especially talented in the arts," continued the visitor.

Her listener nodded understandingly.

"Some day Nestrelda will marry nobility and great wealth, so of course I could not permit my daughter to be associated with you."

"I have high ideals, too, Mrs. Joslin," Nancy stated staunchly.

"You are entirely too conceited to appeal to me," snapped the older woman crossly.

"I really cannot understand your attitude," Nancy said, trying not to show how deeply she had been hurt. "The headmistress invited me——"

"She made an unfortunate mistake," Mrs. Joslin interrupted. "However, as you appear to be a fairly reasonable person, everything can be arranged. You will cancel your reservation at once, Miss Drew."

"I am a reasonable person," Nancy replied quietly. "In fact, I am so reasonable that I believe in justice to myself. I have no intention of giving up the trip."

The woman looked startled, as indeed she was, for she had assumed that the girl would be bluffed easily.

"You will not need to give up the trip," she

said in a milder tone. "You could take another boat."

"For that matter, so could your daughter."

"I prefer to have Nestrelda travel with her school friends."

"And I choose to travel with those girls too," said Nancy spiritedly.

"Then you refuse to do as I request?"

"I am afraid so, Mrs. Joslin. Your attitude doesn't seem reasonable."

"You are an impertinent, ill-mannered girl!" the woman cried, turning away abruptly. "I shouldn't have wasted time talking with you. I'll arrange everything with the headmistress."

Mrs. Joslin reached for her purse and gloves which she had dropped on a chair. Unnoticed until that moment, Snowball had curled herself on the cushion. One of the gloves lay between her paws.

"Horrid creature!" exclaimed the woman, giving the cat a push. "Now my glove is covered with white hair! O—oh!"

Her words ended in a scream of pain. The pet, annoyed by the rough treatment, had made a quick thrust with her paw, scratching Mrs. Joslin across the left cheek as she bent over the chair.

"F—tt, f—tt," Snowball hissed, making another attack, this time tearing the skin on the woman's wrist.

Mrs. Joslin backed away from the chair, a

handkerchief pressed to her face. "My cheek!" she moaned. "I'll be scarred for life! And a cat scratch is dangerous. I may get some dreadful disease."

Nancy rescued Snowball, who became quiet in her arms. The girl tried to apologize, but Mrs. Joslin would not listen. Slamming the door behind her, she ran out to her car and ordered the chauffeur to drive away quickly.

"Oh, dear," Nancy sighed as she watched from the window. "I'm sorry that happened. Now she'll try to cause no end of trouble."

"It was all her own fault," declared Hannah Gruen, who had overheard the conversation. "Yes, Snowball never would have scratched her if she hadn't been annoyed."

"That woman should talk about ill-mannered people!" the housekeeper went on indignantly. "Why, I never saw such an ill-bred person in all my life."

"She seems to have a great idea of her own importance," said Nancy. "I wonder if she really has any influence with the headmistress?"

Later in the afternoon, when George and Bess called, Nancy reported the incident to them.

"I guess I'm not such a desirable person," she said ruefully. "It never occurred to me before that anyone would regard me as unfit company simply because I have solved a few mysteries!"

"And no one does," George declared instantly. "Why, you're the envy of the town.

Mrs. Joslin is just jealous because you have had so much publicity. There isn't a finer, nicer girl in River Heights than you, Nancy.''

"Nor one with higher social qualifications,'' added Bess heartily. "Who is this Nestrelda anyway? I'll venture she hasn't a single friend at Laurel Hall.''

"I believe her mother wouldn't be of much help in making them,'' laughed Nancy. "But I have an uneasy feeling about the trip. The Joslins probably have money, and money does talk, you know.''

"Now don't you worry,'' Bess said comfortingly. "Your passage has been booked, so of course you'll go.''

To make Nancy forget the unpleasant interview, the girls deliberately changed the subject. Before long she was telling them about her latest "case,'' and the request which her father had made regarding the Trentons.

"I'm not sure just what Dad wants me to do yet,'' she admitted to her chums. "However, I think he expects me to become acquainted with Doris and try to make her change her mind.''

"Do you know the Trentons?'' George inquired curiously.

"I met Mrs. Trenton nearly a year ago. She seemed nice, although I talked with her only a minute. I have an idea, girls! Why don't we run out there now?''

"What excuse could we give there for our call?'' asked Bess.

"Oh, we'll think up something. I'll just say that Dad had spoken of Doris so many times, I'd like to meet her."

George and Bess agreed to the plan. Twenty minutes later found them in the Marvin automobile, drawing up before an imposing three-story stone dwelling. The girls crossed a well-tended grass lawn and rang the bell. After a long wait the door was opened by a butler.

"Is this the Trenton home?" inquired Nancy doubtfully.

"Yes," the man responded politely, "but Miss Doris is not at home this afternoon."

"Oh," murmured Nancy in disappointment, "then perhaps Mrs. Trenton will see us."

The butler seemed to hesitate and half inclined his head as if to gaze back over his shoulder. Nancy imagined she could hear a woman crying in one of the nearby rooms.

"Mrs. Trenton is unable to see any visitors today," said the man. "She is indisposed. Will you leave your card?"

"I haven't one with me," replied Nancy, turning away. "We will call again."

As the girls walked back to the car she asked Bess and George if they had heard the sound of weeping from the direction of the living room.

"Yes, I did," declared Bess. "Do you suppose Mrs. Trenton is really ill?"

"It's my opinion she is upset over the actions of her daughter," Nancy responded, climbing into the car. "She probably wasn't in a mood to see anyone, and Doris may have done something today which hurt her.''

As the hour was growing late, the girls drove toward their homes. In passing an intersection at one of the neighborhood business districts, Nancy suddenly craned her neck to gaze at a large limousine parked at the curbing.

''Do you see someone you know?'' questioned George curiously.

''Girls, look there,'' Nancy urged. ''That is Mrs. Joslin's car.''

Bess stopped her machine for a traffic light and turned her head to gaze back. The woman sat alone in the rear seat, but she seemed to be waiting for someone. She kept tapping her pocketbook nervously, and glanced at her wrist watch frequently.

Before the light turned green a thin man with a felt hat pulled low over his eyes came hurriedly from a jewelry store. Mrs. Joslin swung open the car door and he stepped inside. Then the limousine pulled away from the curb, made an illegal turn in the street, and drove off in the opposite direction.

''Surely he isn't her husband,'' remarked Bess thoughtfully. ''He looked years younger than she.''

''I didn't like his appearance at all,'' George declared with emphasis. ''Or hers either, for that matter.''

''I am afraid I prejudiced you against Mrs. Joslin,'' commented Nancy as Bess drove on again. "Probably I shouldn't have been so outspoken."

"On the contrary, you were far too charitable," said George feelingly. "She looks like an old shrew to me."

"Do you know, I've been thinking," remarked Bess slowly. "Seeing these two together, both of them people we don't like, makes me wonder——"

"Makes you wonder what?" George demanded as her cousin hesitated.

"Do you suppose there could be any reason except false pride for Mrs. Joslin not wanting Nancy to travel on the same boat with her daughter?"

The question startled the other two girls.

"I never even thought of such a possibility," Nancy acknowledged. "Just what do you mean, Bess?"

"Mrs. Joslin may be pretending to dislike your ability as a detective because she is afraid of it!"

"Perhaps that's why she's trying to keep you off the boat, Nancy," added George with sudden conviction. "She has something to hide and she doesn't want you to pry into her secrets!"

CHAPTER IV

A Surprise

Nancy was rather impressed by the opinions of her chums. That evening she repeated them to her father at the dinner table.

"Oh, I shouldn't give Mrs. Joslin any more thought," he said carelessly. "I promise you'll sail on the *Patrician* according to schedule. In fact, there is a special reason why you must take that boat."

"The Trenton case?" Nancy inquired eagerly.

"Yes, Nancy, Mrs. Trenton and her daughter are sailing on the *Patrician*. I very foolishly told Mr. Trenton you were taking the same steamer and would do what you could to help Doris."

"My ideas might not agree with those of her parents."

"Mr. Trenton thinks his daughter may elope with some man other than young Washburn. He's bundling her off to South America, hoping to keep her safe, but even so he's afraid the girl may run off or do something rash just to spite him."

"I don't see what I can do about it, Dad."

"Meet the young woman, become friendly

with her, have heart to heart talks with her, and give sensible advice. She may accept it from you when she wouldn't from her parents. You see what I mean?"

"I see," said Nancy dryly, "but I don't like the assignment at all. I thought you were going to give me another mystery case."

"No mysteries on this trip," laughed her father. "For once in your life you'll leave them behind and really enjoy a vacation."

As the telephone rang, Nancy arose to answer it.

"Let me speak to Miss Drew," said a gruff voice. "Miss Nancy Drew."

"This is she speaking."

"Then listen," went on the man harshly, "don't sail on the *Patrician* next week if you know what's wise! That's all, but remember!"

Nancy hung up the receiver and faced her father.

"Who was that?" he asked, rising from the table.

"I don't know," Nancy replied grimly, "but I have an idea." She repeated the warning message.

"I'll try to trace the call," Mr. Drew said angrily.

His efforts were useless, for the telephone operator told him the call had been made from a public phone booth.

"Nancy, had you ever heard the voice before?" the lawyer questioned her.

"No, Dad, but it's my guess the man was Mrs. Joslin's husband, or perhaps the fellow I saw her with today. Who else would be interested in whether or not I sail on the boat?"

"I don't like this business in the least, Nancy. Possibly it would be better if you were to change boats."

"Why Dad! The very idea! I'm not afraid of the Joslins. Anyway, if I don't sail on the *Patrician* I'll not be able to help Doris Trenton."

"Well, we'll see," replied Mr. Drew, frowning. "I'll try to look into this matter before your boat leaves."

The following day Nancy went on with her plans as if nothing had occurred. She spent half a day shopping with Bess and George for cruise clothes. While her chums were trying on dresses she found time to write a note of inquiry to the Motor Vehicle Department of the State, requesting the name of the person who owned a car with the registration number on the envelope and posted it in the store's letter box.

"I hope I get quick action," she told herself. "Otherwise I'll not be able to learn the identity of that young man until I get back from South America. And I must return his fifty dollars."

That afternoon Nancy determined to clear up another matter that worried her. Telling no one of her destination, she set out alone for the factory of Trenton and Washburn, manufacturers of fine luggage. The building, an imposing structure covering half a block, was located at the south side of River Heights.

After trying several entrances the girl came to the main one and entered the office. An indolent young woman allowed her to wait several minutes before inquiring her business.

"I should like to see Mr. Trenton, please."

"Have you an appointment?"

"No, I haven't, but I thought——"

"Not a chance to see him without an appointment," the clerk interrupted. "Mr. Trenton is very busy."

"My father is an old friend of his. If you will tell him I am here——"

"Mr. Trenton doesn't like to be bothered at this time of day," the girl said with finality. "Telephone early tomorrow morning."

Nancy turned away, feeling irritated at the treatment she had received. She reflected that if customers were not given a more polite reception, the business of Trenton and Washburn soon would be on the decline.

"Maybe I can find the man myself," she thought.

Passing another open door, Nancy gazed inside curiously. Before her was a room whose walls were lined solidly with trunks and suitcases. Before she could enter it, a package truck came rushing down the hall, nearly colliding with her.

"Say, can't you keep out of the way?" demanded the boy who pushed it. "You've no business to be here."

"I'm not doing any harm. I merely came to inquire for Mr. Trenton."

"Orders are orders. None but employees are allowed in this section of the building. Now get out and stay out!"

"Oh, very well," Nancy said with a shrug. To herself she added, "I'm going to see Mr. Trenton. How can I do what Dad wants me to unless I meet Doris's father and find out what he's like?"

She retreated down the hall, but as soon as the boy had wheeled his package truck out of sight, she promptly returned. Walking into the storage room and finding nothing there to hold her interest, she moved on to an adjoining one. Suddenly, hearing voices through a door, she halted.

"I tell you, Trenton, this has gone far enough," came to her ears. "I'm not going to keep on paying fancy prices for inferior stuff!"

Nancy moved closer to the wall, instantly guessing that a customer was berating Mr. Trenton for having sold him luggage of questionable quality. She could not catch the factory owner's response since he spoke in a low tone, but the other man's words reached her clearly.

"When your partner Washburn was alive,

there wasn't any of this sort of thing! A customer got what he paid for! The name Trenton and Washburn stamped on a piece of luggage meant something in those days!"

A telephone rang at an empty desk in the opposite corner of the room where Nancy was standing. Fearing that someone would come to answer it and find her there, the girl reluctantly fled into the hall.

"I wish I might have heard more," she thought regretfully. "One thing is perfectly clear, however; Mr. Trenton is resorting to questionable methods in carrying on his business. He is trading upon the name of the firm and charging high prices, yet putting out a poor grade of merchandise."

When her father came home late that afternoon Nancy lost no time in reporting her discovery. As she expected, he found it difficult to believe his client had resorted to dishonorable business practices.

"Trenton must be hard pressed, or he wouldn't cheapen his line of luggage," Mr. Drew declared. "Well, I must say I am surprised. His actions throw a different light on everything."

"In the end, your sympathies may do a right-about-face," predicted Nancy with a wise nod of her head. "I can't help but think that Doris has good reasons for refusing to marry Henry Washburn."

"From something Mr. Trenton said," replied Carson Drew, "I did get an idea that money might be behind it all."

As the doorbell rang, Nancy hurried to answer it.

"It's for me," she called.

"Ned?" inquired her father with a tolerant smile.

"We're going somewhere to eat, then to a picture show, I guess," Nancy explained carelessly. "He asked me over a week ago to be sure and save tonight for him."

"Have a good time," Mr. Drew called after her.

Ned glanced critically at Nancy's high-heeled pumps as she met him at the door.

"Better change those," he advised with masculine bluntness.

"But why, Ned? If we're going to a show——"

"Maybe we aren't," the young man replied mysteriously.

"Hurry up and get into a pair with low heels. We're late now."

"Late for what?" questioned Nancy.

"Oh, you'll find out," Ned told her, grinning broadly.

After Nancy obediently changed her shoes, the two set out in the young man's car. Ned took a road which led to the outskirts of River Heights.

"What is all the mystery anyway?" Nancy

asked suspiciously. "Am I being kidnapped?"

"That's right," laughed Ned. "We're here now."

He whirled the steering wheel and the car rolled into Grantwell Park. At long benches in the grove Nancy caught a glimpse of some twenty or thirty young people.

"It's a steak roast," explained Ned, parking the car. "We're giving it as a sort of farewell for you and Bess and George."

"Oh, Ned, how nice!"

"Well, I don't know," the boy said disparagingly. "The steaks may be pretty tough. I picked 'em out. And it looks as if a storm is kicking up." He glanced at the sky where heavy clouds had begun to erase the light.

"Oh, it won't rain, Ned. We won't let it!"

Springing from the car, Nancy ran to meet her friends. Bess and George already were there. They confessed that the farewell picnic had been a surprise to them also.

The young people built fires in the stoves provided for the purpose, made a hot drink, and cooked sizzling steaks which disappeared as rapidly as they came from the pans.

"Oh, this has been a wonderful picnic!" Nancy declared as she finished her third sandwich. "Ned, I have never tasted better meat."

"I was right about the storm at any rate," he returned, once more studying the inky sky above the electric lights which had been turned on, "That rain isn't going to pass over."

"Oughtn't we to be starting home?" suggested Bess nervously. "I don't like to break up the party, but it may be hard to drive in a heavy rain."

The others agreed that it would be wise to bring the picnic to a speedy end. Hampers were loaded into the cars and the grounds were cleaned of papers and refuse.

"We've waited just a few minutes too long," Ned declared, dousing water on the fire. "The storm is going to beat us home."

A few of the cars began to pull away from the park. Nancy and Bess were still gathering up stray papers when a strong breath of wind rustled the tree leaves overhead.

"It's coming!" cried Bess, starting to run for the car.

Even as she spoke, a flash of lightning severed the clouds. Instantly the park illuminating system went out of order.

"Nancy!" shouted Ned in alarm, for in the darkness he could not see her.

"Hurry!" screamed Bess. "Don't bother about the rest of those papers."

"Coming," called Nancy, but her voice was drowned by a loud roar of thunder.

At the same instant the ground for many yards about was brilliantly lighted. Close to the shelter house not far from where Nancy had been standing, a great tree shivered and splintered from a mighty impact.

"Wow! That was close!" cried Ned. "A bolt of lightning must have struck it!"

"Nancy! Nancy! Are you all right?" shouted Bess.

There was no answering call even when the others joined in the cry. In horror the young people leaped toward the spot where the girl last had been seen.

CHAPTER V

A Bolt of Lightning

Groping about in the darkness, the picnickers stumbled upon Nancy lying in a crumpled heap on the grass.

"She's been struck by lightning," wailed Bess, dropping down on her knees before the unconscious girl.

"Speak to us!" sobbed George, beside herself with fear.

Nancy moved slightly, murmuring, "Where —am—I? What—happened?"

The young people were so relieved to hear their friend's voice that they could have shouted for joy. Ned picked up the girl in his arms and carried her to the car.

"We must get a doctor right away," urged George. "Drive as fast as you can, Ned."

"I'm all right," Nancy maintained weakly, trying to sit up. "I was stunned for a minute when that tree was struck. My mind is clearing now. Just take me home."

Ned and the girls felt that she should be overruled, but Nancy won out in the end. She insisted upon returning to the Drew house. Before River Heights was reached she was much

better, but all agreed that her escape from
death had been miraculous.

Mr. Drew and Hannah Gruen shared the same
thought when they learned of the accident.
Despite Nancy's protests, they put her to bed at
once. After sleeping well throughout the night,
she awakened with only a slight headache to remind her of the misadventure.

Nancy had finished eating a late breakfast
and was packing a few articles into her new
trunk when Hannah came upstairs to tell her
she had a caller.

"It's Senora Zola, headmistress of Laurel
Hall," whispered the housekeeper.

Nancy tossed a pair of stockings into the
trunk. "Oh, dear, I was afraid of this."

Wondering if Mrs. Joslin had succeeded in
causing trouble, the girl went downstairs to
meet the headmistress. A prim woman in her
late thirties looked decidedly ill at ease as she
took Nancy's hand.

"I must apologize for calling in the morning," she began nervously in a delightful low
voice with a slight accent. "I really had to talk
with you about your plans for the trip to Buenos
Aires. I—I scarcely know how to say what is in
my mind."

"Perhaps I can help you," said Nancy, taking pity upon the lady. "Mrs. Joslin came to
see me yesterday."

"Oh, then you know why I am here?"

"Mrs. Joslin made several mean accusations

against me. No doubt she repeated them to you."

"Yes, she did, Nancy. Needless to say, I consider her attitude very unreasonable. You can understand I am placed in a most difficult position. Nestrelda is a student in our school, and her parents are influential."

"I quite understand, Senora Zola. Then you wish me to withdraw from the trip?"

The headmistress could not conceal her feeling of relief. "It would simplify matters if you should decide to join another group, Nancy. I realize I have no right to make such a request when the trip is only four days away. Will it greatly upset you to change?"

"I had planned on traveling aboard the *Patrician*," Nancy said honestly. "Of course, I am disappointed."

While the two sat discussing the situation, Bess and George arrived at the Drew home. Nancy immediately introduced them to the headmistress, who again reviewed Mrs. Joslin's demand.

"I've never heard of such a request," Bess declared indignantly. "Nancy is a wonderful girl and I'm sure she is as—as cultured as Mrs. Joslin's daughter!"

"I quite agree," the headmistress returned, smiling. "I am afraid Nestrelda's mother is rather narrow-minded."

"If Nancy isn't to be allowed to make the voyage, Bess and I also will withdraw,'' George announced flatly.

"I do not blame you. If you senoritas wish to take another boat, I shall be very glad to redeem the boat tickets."

"But it is so late to change our plans now," protested Bess.

"Yes, it is," admitted the distressed woman. "I promised Mrs. Joslin I would speak to Nancy about the matter. However, if you young ladies feel that you cannot change to another boat, I shall not insist upon it."

"It may cost you a great deal if we do make the trip," stated Nancy.

Senora Zola nodded. "I haven't told you everything. Mrs. Joslin is my half sister. For the past three years she has contributed heavily to the support of the school."

"I see," said Nancy. "You are placed in an awkward position."

The caller began to pull on her gloves, avoiding the girl's steady gaze. "When may I have your decision, Nancy?" she asked nervously.

"I'll talk with my father and let you know early tomorrow."

"Do tell him how sorry I am," the headmistress murmured as the girl walked with her to the door. "I was so upset about the matter that I scarcely slept last night."

After the woman had left, the three chums gave expression to their feelings. However, provoked as they were over the request, they could not really blame the cultured headmistress, who had come from South America to take charge of the delightful school. They liked the woman, and realized she was dominated by her half sister, whose money was needed to support Laurel Hall

"I think it wouldn't be much fun traveling with Nestrelda in any case," declared George with a toss of her head "I wish we could go alone."

"So do I," replied Nancy soberly. "Let's talk over the matter with our parents."

Mr. Drew, the Marvins and the Faynes found it difficult to arrive at a decision. They agreed that the girls would have a more enjoyable trip traveling unchaperoned, yet they did not wish to send them on such a trip without an older woman in the group.

"We don't know a person who is going to South America," Bess said gloomily.

Thoughtfully Nancy sat stroking Snowball's soft fur. Then suddenly she cried out:

"Oh, girls, something has just come to me! I've been trying and trying to figure out who might have sent this cat to me, and I believe I've hit upon the answer!"

"What has that to do with our present problem?" demanded George in a despairing voice.

"Why, everything! Do you remember that darling little lady from Buenos Aires whom I kept from being swindled?"

"Mrs. Purdy?" cried Bess, becoming interested. "She was crazy about cats!"

"Mrs. Purdy often said she was thinking of returning to South America on a visit after her husband died," Nancy went on. "You recall she was born there but married a man from our country. Possibly we could induce her to travel as our chaperon."

"She would be a very suitable person," declared Mrs. Marvin, when she heard the suggestion. "I would not hesitate sending Bess with her. She is a most delightful person, and speaks her native tongue so beautifully."

Since Mrs. Purdy was favored by everyone, Nancy and her chums set off at once toward the woman's home which was located in the town of Weldon, not far from River Heights. Presently they came to a charming little vine-covered cottage at the east edge of the village.

"This must be the place," said Bess, adding in disappointment, "The windows are boarded up. She must have gone away."

"Mrs. Purdy was our only hope," groaned George, her shoulders slumping. "Now what are we to do?"

Nancy climbed from the car. "Let's inquire at the next house to make certain we have found the right place."

A motherly woman in pink gingham, who came to the door, expressed a kindly sympathy when the girls told her why they wished to locate her neighbor.

"Now isn't that too bad?" she murmured. "Mrs. Purdy closed up her cottage not three days ago. She went back to South America to visit her folks."

"And to think we might have gone with her if only we had known!" exclaimed Bess, visibly wilting.

"I don't suppose you have Mrs. Purdy's address?" Nancy inquired after a long moment of silence.

"Why yes, I have it. She asked me to write to her. Would you care to have it?"

"Please."

The woman disappeared into the house, returning in a moment with a slip of paper which she gave to Nancy.

"I don't see what good her address will do us," Bess complained listlessly as the chums got into the car. "Mrs. Purdy is probably on board ship by this time."

"Oh, I meant to ask that woman the name of the steamer she sailed on!" Nancy exclaimed, running to the porch to correct her oversight.

After learning that the woman had traveled on the *Coronda,* the girl also inquired if she owned a large white cat.

"Mrs. Purdy did have one, a handsome creature," declared the lady in the pink gingham. "She decided not to take it with her to Buenos Aires."

"What became of the cat?" Nancy asked quickly.

"She told me she gave it to a girl who had befriended her at one time. I never did hear the young lady's name."

Nancy might have set the woman's mind at rest upon that point; instead, she thanked her for the information and returned excitedly to her waiting chums.

"Now we're going to the nearest telegraph office," she told them cheerfully. "It may be a waste of good money, but I intend to send a radiogram to Mrs. Purdy's ship."

"Asking her to come back home?" asked Bess teasingly.

"We'll request her to serve as our chaperon after we reach Buenos Aires. Maybe she'll do it, and if she should consent, our parents surely won't object to our traveling alone."

"That's a wonderful idea, Nancy!" said George with sudden approval.

At the Weldon telegraph office another customer stood in line ahead of the girls. They were compelled to wait until he had written his message as he was using the only available pencil. To their annoyance he seemed unable to make up his mind what he wished to say. Finally he tore off the sheet from the pad and tossed it carelessly toward the waste basket. The paper missed its mark, but the man did not notice this as he busied himself with writing a second message.

"We'll be here all day," Bess sighed, shifting her weight from one foot to the other.

Nancy could not see the man's face clearly, for it was half hidden beneath a wide-brimmed felt hat. She had a feeling that she had met him before somewhere. Without glancing toward the girls, he shoved his completed message and a crisp bill across the desk, then left the building.

"Thank goodness," sighed Bess. "Now it's our turn to use the pencil."

To the surprise of her chums Nancy crossed to the waste basket and picked up from the floor the piece of paper dropped by the stranger. As she started to throw it into the nearby receptacle, she noticed the message written on the sheet. A strange expression came over her face.

"What's the matter?" inquired George, moving quickly to her chum's side.

"Just read this," said Nancy in awe. "'Drew La Plata Saturday.' Now what can that mean with my name in it?"

CHAPTER VI

THE SECRET CODE

"THE message does contain your name, Nancy!" agreed George as she read the paper.

"And the day of our intended sailing to South America," added Bess, likewise astonished. "But where does the La Plata come in?"

"I can't figure it out," George responded, looking troubled. "Maybe we are all involved."

"I wish I had a map," murmured Nancy thoughtfully as she smoothed a stray hair.

"How would that help?" inquired Bess.

Nancy smiled. "This message refers either to a person or to a place. It must be written in code."

"Oh, perhaps it doesn't concern you at all," George spoke carelessly. "You have never seen the man before in your life, have you?"

"I'm not sure. His face was half hidden beneath the hat brim, but I did think he looked somewhat familiar."

"And I had the same feeling," declared Bess.

"Oh, girls, now I remember!" Nancy exclaimed in a low tone. "Wasn't he the man we saw getting into Mrs. Joslin's car?"

"At the jewelry store!" agreed George instantly.

"I believe he was that man," added Bess, although with less conviction. "In that case, Nancy, this message might concern you. Didn't I say Mrs. Joslin had a very special reason for trying to keep you from sailing on the same boat as her daughter?"

"Yes, you did, Bess." Nancy slipped the paper into her purse. "I mean to show this message to Dad and see what he thinks of it."

After sending off a cable to Mrs. Purdy, the girls returned to River Heights. Nancy stopped for a few minutes at her father's law office, but was disappointed because he did not appear greatly impressed with the message she had found in the telegraph office.

"I fail to comprehend how it can have any connection with you," he told her. "However, I am glad that by not sailing with the Laurel Hall girls, you will have nothing more to do with the Joslins."

"I wonder if I'll be sailing at all," said Nancy, submerged in gloom. "Mrs. Purdy is our only hope now. She may not even get my radiogram."

Bess and George were waiting in the car. When Nancy returned, looking very glum, they suggested a shopping trip, an idea which was promptly turned down.

"I'm in no mood for it today. Besides, I must go directly home. Hannah is head over heels in work and I promised to assist her.''

"We'll pitch in too," Bess offered as the car took them to the Drew home. "I'm experienced at packing trunks."

As the girls ran up the front steps of the Drew home, Nancy noticed a battered vehicle standing on the driveway. She surmised that Mrs. Gruen had called in Effie, a willing but somewhat stupid maid who often did day's work for the Drews. Upon entering the house, they were confronted with a great cloud of dust which made them cough and choke. Effie was sweeping the carpet with a broom.

"I really think you should use the vacuum," explained Nancy patiently.

"Oh, all right," the maid grumbled good-naturedly, "but I never did like them electric contraptions. They're always out of whack."

"Effie!" called Hannah Gruen from the next room.

"Yes'm."

"Never mind the cleaning," the housekeeper told her wearily. "It will be better for me to take care of it myself. Can you sew?"

"Yes'm, I'm a right good hand with a needle."

"Then I'll have you finish shortening Nancy's dresses," Mrs. Gruen said, indicating a pile of garments on the dining room table. "Take off exactly three inches from each hem. But don't touch this pink skirt; I've done that."

"Is there anything I can do?" Nancy inquired

after the housekeeper had repeated her instructions to be certain the maid understood.

"When Effie finishes, I'll want you to try on the garments. In the meantime you might vacuum the floor while I go to the grocery store."

The three girls made quick work of the first floor cleaning. When they went upstairs to Nancy's room, her chums were surprised to see her start hunting through her bookcase.

"What in the world are you doing?" asked Bess. "I thought we were going to help you pack."

"Just a moment," answered the Drew girl. "I must hunt up something first."

"I bet you are looking for a map," surmised George.

"Exactly," responded Nancy. "I believe I'll solve that code yet."

" 'Drew La Plata Saturday,' " recited Bess. "Do you suppose it's the name of a sister boat?"

"No," said her chum. "I believe it is a river, but I must verify it."

Quickly she opened an atlas. Hastily turning the pages she read, "La Plata Rio. Buenos Aires is on the river La Plata which flows into the ocean."

"Nancy Drew!" gasped her friends in unison. "You're a real detective!"

The girls fell to discussing the case from various angles, so failed to notice Effie lay several garments on the bed. Suddenly Nancy looked at the pink skirt, wondering if she dared believe her eyes. Quickly slipping on the garment, she was dismayed to discover that it came far above her knees and flared out at a ridiculous angle.

"See what Effie has done! She must have shortened this skirt after Mrs. Gruen told her to leave it alone!"

"You'll create a sensation if you wear that on the boat!" giggled Bess mischievously.

"It looks like a circus rider's costume," added George, laughing gleefully. "All you need is a horse, Nancy."

"This isn't a bit funny, girls." Anxiously the Drew girl examined the skirt hem and was relieved to find that Effie had not cut it off. "Well, thank goodness for that. I'll rip it out and not tell Hannah. Poor woman, she has enough to worry her."

Throughout the day Effie made several other mistakes so that by six o'clock when she received her wages and departed, the housekeeper actually heaved a sigh of relief.

"Another day like this and I'll spend my vacation in a sanitarium," she declared wildly.

While Nancy and her father were at dinner that evening, with Ned Nickerson as their guest, a radiogram arrived from Mrs. Purdy. As Nancy tore open the envelope, she wondered with a thumping heart if the contents would be good news.

"Hurrah!" she cried in a moment. "We can go!"

The woman had sent word she planned to spend several months in Buenos Aires and would be delighted to have the three girls with her. She also acknowledged that she had given Snowball to Nancy, and considered the girl clever to have traced the gift.

"Then this settles everything," Mr. Drew said in satisfaction. "I'll leave for the West feeling that you will be in safe hands, Nancy."

Ned said nothing at all. His opinion was that a chaperon would not prevent Nancy from finding adventure in South America. Later that evening, when she showed him the mysterious radiogram she had picked up from the floor of the telegraph office, he shook his head morosely.

"You're always running into grief, Nancy. Take my advice and don't bother with any dark and wily strangers. I would have nothing to do with the Trenton case, the Joslins, or anyone else if I were in your shoes."

"Ned, you're turning into a regular grandpa," Nancy teased him. "How about driving me to the Trentons right now? I should like to meet Doris before we sail."

Rather unwillingly he agreed to take her. However, before they could leave the house, an automobile turned into the driveway. Observing it, the young people waited on the front porch. To Nancy's amazement Mrs. Joslin alighted and crossed the lawn.

"Good evening," said the Drew girl politely. "Will you come in?"

"No, I'll state what I have to say right here. I understand Senora Zola came to see you and that you gave her no definite answer about your trip."

"That is true," replied Nancy, rather enjoying the situation.

"You must make up your mind at once!" the woman said arrogantly. "Do you realize that the boat sails Saturday?"

"So it does."

"Unless you withdraw from the Laurel Hall group I shall take Nestrelda out of school there," Mrs. Joslin threatened. "I'll protest to the steamship authorities——"

"Please compose yourself," suggested Nancy calmly. "You will not have to worry about this affair any more. I have decided not to travel with the Laurel Hall girls."

"You might have said so before!" Mrs. Joslin snapped.

Without a word of gratitude, the woman turned and hastened back to her car; in fact, she left so quickly that Nancy had no time to say anything further. In no uncertain words Ned voiced his opinion of Mrs. Joslin. He also prophesied that when the woman should learn Nancy and her friends were sailing on the

Patrician she would attempt to make trouble.

"She won't know it for a while," Nancy laughed, undisturbed, as the two drove off. "Anyway, I'm not in the least afraid of Mrs. Joslin or her daughter Nestrelda."

Arriving at the Trenton Home, Nancy and Ned were surprised at the greeting received from the family. The father, a tired looking man with spectacles, had very little to say. His wife, a quiet, subdued lady with snow white hair, tried rather pathetically to make conversation. It was Doris, perfectly poised and sure of herself, who responded to Nancy's casual remarks. Mr. and Mrs. Trenton became increasingly ill at ease as the conversation shifted to the topic of their daughter's trip to South America.

"I am going mostly because Mother and Father wish me to," the girl said with a shrug. "I really can't arouse much enthusiasm for the voyage."

"Oh, I'm sure we'll have a wonderful time," Nancy declared enthusiastically.

A puzzled expression passed over Miss Trenton's face.

"Are you going to Buenos Aires also?" she asked quietly.

"Why yes, I thought you knew. We're sailing on the same boat."

For an instant Doris Trenton lost her poise. A half frightened expression came into her dark eyes. She turned to regard her parents with a fixed gaze which was difficult to interpret.

"No, I didn't know," she replied as if speaking to Nancy. "How delightful. How very delightful."

CHAPTER VII

THE INTRUDER

DORIS'S words had been spoken in a half mocking tone, so Nancy instantly gathered that the young woman had guessed her mission. Conversation became increasingly stilted and difficult. Soon the young people excused themselves and left the house.

Nancy might have dismissed the matter from her mind, had not a letter arrived the next morning from the Motor Vehicle Department of the state. In response to her inquiry, she was informed that the car which had struck her coupe was registered in the name of Doris Trenton!

"If that isn't the strangest thing yet!" Nancy exclaimed aloud. "That changes a lot of things."

With time so pressing it was out of the question for her to visit the Trenton home again, so she decided to wait and question the young woman. However, as chance had it she encountered Doris scarcely an hour later in the Red Lion Tea Room, where both girls were lunching after last-minute shopping trips.

Miss Trenton sat at a table in one corner of the crowded dining room, unaware that she was being observed. Nancy saw her take a small photograph from her purse and stare at it intently.

Choosing that moment, the Drew girl left her own table and glided to Doris's side. Hastily the young woman covered the picture, but not before Nancy glimpsed the face. She thought she recognized a likeness of the red-haired man whose car had damaged her own.

"Oh, hello," Miss Trenton said nervously. "Won't you sit down?"

Nancy slid into the empty seat. After a few casual remarks she took the letter from the Motor Vehicle Department out of her purse and handed it to Doris.

"What is this, Miss Drew?"

"Read it, please. I think you will understand."

As she scanned the letter, the young woman's face flushed a delicate pink.

"I own such a car," she admitted slowly, "but why should you make this inquiry?"

Briefly Nancy gave an account of her meeting with the red-haired chap, all the while watching Doris closely. She could see that the girl was deeply embarrassed.

"I—I—the person you mention did use my car," Doris admitted unwillingly. "The young man may have struck your coupe, but since you say he paid you for the damage, I would forget about it if I were you."

"I owe him fifty dollars, Miss Trenton. The

garage bill came to only half of what he gave me."

"He must have intended that you keep it all." Miss Trenton avoided Nancy's penetrating glance. "Don't worry about it."

"Really, I can't help it. I feel duty bound to return the money. Can't you give me the young man's address?"

"Oh, no! I can't even tell you his name. Please, just forget about it, Miss Drew. Keep the fifty dollars."

Murmuring an excuse, the young woman hastily paid her bill and fled from the tea room.

"She did know the name of that young man," Nancy told herself. "How foolish of her to think she could deceive me! She's hiding something, and I mean to find out more about it."

Gathering up her packages, the girl took a cab home. She found the household in a greater flurry than usual, for at three o'clock Carson Drew would catch a plane for the West. Nancy helped pack his suitcases and accompanied him to the airport.

"I don't like to leave before you do, Nancy," Mr. Drew told his daughter regretfully. "But you understand how it is. I must be in Salt Lake City by Friday night."

"I'll get along all right by myself, Dad."

"I am sure you will or I shouldn't leave. Now you have your passport, your money—everything."

"Yes, Dad, don't worry about me. Everything will be fine."

A giant three-motored transport plane taxied down the runway, drawing up in front of the passenger station. Hurriedly Mr. Drew kissed his daughter good-bye, but could not refrain from adding a final word of advice.

"Be sure to take good care of your passport while you are away, Nancy. If you should lose it, you might get into endless trouble."

"I'll be careful, Dad."

Nancy watched her father board the plane, and remained as the great ship soared westward. Realizing that she would not see him for many months, a deep pang of loneliness struck her. The feeling quickly passed, however, and as she sped from the airport in a cab she again began making plans for her own trip.

On the way home Nancy stopped at a pet store to buy a specially constructed cage in which she could take Snowball aboard the boat. She smiled as she recalled Hannah Gruen's pointed comments upon the subject of cats. The housekeeper remained firmly convinced that it would be a serious mistake to take the pet on the ocean.

The last-minute packing of Nancy's attractive wardrobe was yet to be done. Noticing that the girl did not have a suitable clothes-brush and sewing kit, Mrs. Gruen changed her dress to a light silk and hurried toward the nearest stores to make these quite necessary purchases.

It was then that a figure, who had been pretending to knock at the back door as a salesman with a large handbag, placed a skeleton key in the lock, opening his way into the Drew homestead.

"Let me see," he thought quickly. "The second floor is where I'll find my opportunity."

The man hastened upstairs and glanced into a bedroom furnished with mahogany pieces.

"Huh! Carson Drew's outfit," he said at the first doorway, and moved on down the hall.

Pushing open a partly closed door, he recognized, because of its daintiness, the bedroom of a young girl.

"So this is it," he muttered, pushing back his cap slightly.

Opening his large suitcase, he rushed to the clothes closet, grabbed Nancy's neatly pressed new traveling clothes, and hastily placed the garments into the leather case. The sinister intruder laughed softly as he jammed the expensive suits and dresses into the small quarters.

"Guess that'll be O. K. to the boss," the man grunted. "Long as I get my money I should worry about other people's troubles. I s'pose the boss has got some kind of a grudge against the dame."

Taking a large folded paper bag from his pocket, he tossed some more frocks into it.

"She's got right nice things," he commented.

stopping to examine a pretty belt buckle of hand wrought silver.

Meanwhile Nancy, unaware of the state of affairs at home, drove along her street in her taxi cab. Suddenly she spied her housekeeper hurrying toward the house. The Drew girl stopped the cab, paid the driver, and called to Hannah.

"I just did some last-minute shopping for you," the housekeeper explained. "I got a real nice sewing kit. I'm sure you will like it."

Nancy, appreciative of the woman's thoughtfulness, mentioned the fact as the two walked toward the porch. As Nancy unlocked the front door, a strange sound greeted their ears.

"Mercy me!" cried Mrs. Gruen. "Someone has broken in here. Everything is upset."

Nancy rushed to the stairs.

"Wait!" admonished the housekeeper. "Someone dangerous might still be hiding up there."

"I must see who it is," called the girl, as she bounded up the stairs.

One look into her bedroom closet convinced her the intruder must be someone who was determined she should not go on the trip.

"My clothes are gone!" Nancy shouted down to Hannah. "All my very best ones." A wave of defeat seemed to engulf her. "I hardly expected this," she murmured sadly. "My trip is spoiled."

Mrs. Gruen looked about the living room, but

could see no sign of a figure in hiding. Quickly she called police headquarters, from which an officer was dispatched at once.

"The police are coming to investigate," she explained to Nancy. "We'll just leave everything for them to do."

"Not me, Hannah! I must get to the bottom of this myself," replied the girl with spirit. "I'm going to look under everything. Perhaps we scared him too soon for him to get away."

Hastily pulling aside the white drapes which covered the furniture, Nancy hoped for a clue. Suddenly in the dining room she gave a cry of joy.

"Hannah! Look! My blue suit at the window sill!"

Quickly the two searchers peered through the open window. There lay the contents of the suitcase, strewn on the ground. Evidently the fellow had been frightened off. In a large rubbish bin in the garden Nancy unearthed the paper bag of clothing just as an officer arrived.

"Queer business," muttered the policeman, making a note of the various findings. Finally he left, assuring Nancy the house would be guarded carefully during the girl's absence.

Hannah was very nervous, and it took a great deal of soothing on the part of Nancy to get the housekeeper calm enough to start the tremendous task of pressing the garments and packing the trunk for the trip. Effie was called in to help, but was so thrilled with the story she really was of little use, save for minor duties. All this further aggravated Mrs. Gruen. "I declare, it's just one thing after another when you're busy," she said crossly.

Even as she spoke there came a shrill screeching of car brakes in front of the house.

"Now what?" the woman demanded.

Nancy ran to the window. "It's the expressman after my trunk," she reported, "and I haven't locked it yet. Effie, run into the study and bring that heavy sweater I left there, will you, please?"

A tall young man with a preoccupied air leaped from the truck and hurried up the walk. While Nancy and Effie rushed about getting the trunk ready to go, Hannah met him at the door.

"We're not quite ready," she said. "Can you wait a minute?"

"Oh, sure," he replied good-naturedly. "Glad to rest a minute," he added, sitting down on the steps.

Presently he was escorted up the stairs to Nancy's room where the new brass-bound trunk, now locked, stood ready for shipment.

"Pretty swell," commented the young man "Good enough for a limerick. I once won a limerick contest. How's this?" He muttered to himself a moment, then recited:

"A hide-bound trunk; a brass-bound trunk,
  Like the pirates of old in the seaways sunk;
  It looks like a page

From a venturesome age——
But likely as not, it's plumb full of junk!"

"Your guess is better than your poetry,"
Nancy laughed. "It *is* full of junk and heavy
junk at that. Just lift it."

"Oh, this one is light as trunks go," the
young man scoffed. "I can handle it easily."

Nancy told him where to send the luggage and
pocketed the receipt which he gave her. She
then dismissed the matter from her mind as she
busied herself with last-minute tasks.

"I want to mail a letter to Dad," she told
Hannah a little later. "I'll be right back," she
promised, hurrying down the street.

Suddenly her attention was drawn to a taxi
which had stopped for a traffic light. She
paused and stared, hardly daring to believe
what she saw.

In the back seat sat the same red-haired
young man whose car had struck her own!

"Oh, wait!" Nancy called, starting to cross
the street.

The man turned toward her, and she was certain he recognized her at once. In a low voice he
said something to the driver. As the light
flashed green, the cab sped on, rounding a
corner and disappearing in the distance.

Frantically Nancy glanced about, but no other
taxi was at hand. She realized it would be a
waste of time to try to pursue the young man on
foot.

"He deliberately ran away from me," she told herself angrily. "I only wanted to give him the fifty dollars, but evidently he thinks I intend to make trouble for him."

By the time Nancy reached home she found that most of the work of closing the house had been completed. Hannah Gruen was actually enjoying a few minutes of rest.

"Now let me see," the housekeeper murmured. "Is everything ready? Have you your trunk check?"

"Yes, in my purse."

"And your passport?"

"I left it on top of the desk. I'll put it in my pocketbook before I forget."

Nancy went into the next room and was gone several minutes. Finally she reappeared in the doorway, looking troubled.

"Hannah, you didn't pick up my passport this afternoon?"

"Why no, Nancy! Don't tell me it's gone!"

"I was sure I laid it on top of the desk," the girl declared. "It isn't there now."

"Oh, dear, of all things to lose!"

"It must be here somewhere," said Nancy, trying hard to remain calm, but becoming more and more suspicious every minute.

She and the housekeeper searched through the desk and then behind it. Then they took everything from the girl's purse. Finally they looked carefully in every room. The missing passport could not be found!

CHAPTER VIII

The Missing Passport

"Oh, what will you do, Nancy?" moaned Hannah, beside herself with worry. "If you don't find your passport, you'll not be able to sail!"

"I hope that intruder didn't steal it," said Nancy in a shocked voice.

"Oh, goodness, that would be awful," muttered the housekeeper dolefully. "There certainly seems to be a jinx connected with your trip. Maybe we've mislaid the paper after all," she said soothingly.

"Oh, I only hope so," replied the distraught girl.

"Try to think, Nancy. Do you suppose you could have dropped it into your trunk?" Hannah suggested.

"No," said Nancy, shaking her golden curls. "I'm certain I didn't do that."

"The trunk stood open in your room."

"I left it that way so I could put in things at the last minute. But I know I didn't touch the passport."

"You sent Effie to the living room for your

84

sweater," the housekeeper said slowly. "Do you suppose——"

"I remember seeing Effie drop something besides the sweater into the trunk. Oh, maybe it was my passport! I must find the girl at once and ask her."

There followed a never to be forgotten hour of anxiety as Nancy and Hannah made a desperate attempt to locate Effie. A call at her home brought only the vague information that the maid had gone out.

Quickly they went on a tour of the prominent streets of River Heights. Finally, when the two had lost all hope, they chanced upon the girl in a drug store, blissfully drinking a large glass of chocolate soda.

"Oh, Effie, we've found you at last!" Nancy exclaimed.

"Why, have you been looking for me?" inquired the maid innocently.

"Have we been looking for you! Effie, we've searched all over!"

"Oh, I just been walking around, looking in the shop windows."

"Effie," interrupted Mrs. Gruen impatiently, "did you take any papers from the top of the desk?"

"Papers?" the maid asked blankly. "Desk?"

"The one in our study," supplied Nancy. "My passport was lying there."

Light broke over Effie. "Oh, you mean that little book with your picture in it?"

"Yes, did you touch it, Effie?"

"Now lemme think. I put some papers in your trunk because I was afraid you might forget 'em. Maybe that picture thing was in the pile."

"Oh, Effie!" scolded the housekeeper. "Of all the trouble you've caused!"

"Now what have I done?" the maid wailed. "I only meant to help. Didn't you want those papers in the trunk?"

"I certainly did not," Nancy said with emphasis. "But then I'll not blame you because you didn't understand. The important thing now is to stop that trunk and find out if you did put the passport in it, or whether somebody else took it."

Leaving a very bewildered Effie behind, Mrs. Gruen and Nancy set off in a taxi cab for the express office. They found the building closed for the night! Undaunted, Nancy obtained the manager's name and telephoned him at his house, telling of her plight.

"I remember that trunk," the man said after a moment of thought. "Brass-bound, wasn't it?"

"Yes," Nancy declared eagerly, "and my initials, N. D., also were in brass. The trunk must be stopped."

"Sorry, Miss, but it's too late. Your luggage went off to New York this afternoon."

"Oh, dear, what shall I do?" the girl asked in distress. "I must find out if my passport is locked inside the trunk. If I don't get it I'll not be allowed to sail."

"I'll tell you what I'll do," the manager said finally. "I can send a wire to our New York office. I'll ask them to hold the trunk and not put it aboard the *Patrician* until after you have inspected it."

"Oh, thank you!" Nancy cried gratefully. "Will you send the wire right away?"

"I'll take care of it at once. Your trunk will be waiting for you when you reach New York. I suggest you get there as soon as you can. It may take a little time to straighten out matters."

Enroute home Nancy and Hannah discussed the situation. Both were agreed that, considering the emergency, it would be wise for the girl to leave for New York on the midnight train.

"Bess and George may not wish to change their plans," Nancy said anxiously. "If they feel they can't start tonight, then I'll have to go on alone."

However, both girls were willing to hasten their leave-taking by a day. Yet Bess pointed out one objection to the plan which had not occurred to Nancy.

"What shall we do about the farewell party that Mable Arnold is holding in our honor?"

"We'll have to ask her to speed it up," Nancy said regretfully. "We could dance until nearly midnight and then go directly to the train."

In the end it was so arranged. During the

early hours of the night the young people danced and made merry, but promptly at the stroke of eleven-thirty they piled into cars and drove to the railroad station.

A large group, including Hannah Gruen and Effie, had gathered to see the girls on their way. Observing the maid standing alone, Nancy went to speak to her.

"Did you find your passport, Miss Nancy?" Effie inquired. "I been worryin' about it ever since I heard."

"I haven't located the trunk yet, but I expect to get it when I reach New York." She explained nothing further, but her heart became heavy as she thought again of the possibility she might not find the precious paper.

As the train came into the station, Nancy, Bess and George said good-bye to their friends and climbed aboard. Ned helped the porter with their hand luggage and assisted the girls in locating their berths in the Pullman.

"Don't stay too late, Ned," Nancy warned her friend uneasily. "It must be about time for the train to start. You may be taken along."

"I might at that."

Nancy failed to notice the significant tone, for at that moment Effie, her hat at a rakish angle, came running down the aisle.

"Miss Nancy!" she called in an excited voice.

"Effie, what are you doing on the train?"

"Oh, Miss Nancy, I had to tell you! I just

saw the men putting it into the baggage car!"

"What are you talking about, Effie?"

"Your trunk. They're putting it on this very train."

"How can that be?" Nancy murmured in bewilderment. "The manager of the express company told me the trunk had been shipped. You're sure it was mine, Effie?"

"It was a great big trunk with a lot of brass trimming. And your initials were on it too."

Before Effie could say more the train gave a sudden jerk and started to move. With a shriek the woman ran for the vestibule. Ned followed and helped her swing down to the platform. Then he walked back leisurely into the car.

"Ned!" Nancy exclaimed. "Why didn't you get off?"

The young man grinned. "You see, I have a ticket."

He then explained that Carson Drew had asked him to see the girls to their boat.

"And all this time you never said a word about it!"

"You've been so busy I didn't have a chance," Ned defended himself. "Anyway, I thought I would hand myself to you as a nice surprise package."

Effie's loud talking had disturbed many persons who were trying to sleep. As someone called out. "Quiet, please!" the young people lowered their voices. However, they went on conversing in whispers, discussing the news which the maid had brought.

"Effie makes so many mistakes I hardly know whether to believe her or not," Nancy declared. "Still, I can't afford to overlook any possibility. I'll talk with the conductor."

She and Ned found the man in another car. To their request that they be allowed to visit the baggage car, he turned a deaf ear.

"Sorry, it's against the rules," was his gruff reply.

"It would save me so much trouble if only I could get into my trunk tonight," Nancy pleaded with him. "Unless I locate my passport I'll not be able to sail."

"I can't allow you in the baggage car," the conductor repeated, "but since it's so important I'll tell you what I'll do," he added, relenting a little, "I'll go myself and see if the trunk is on the train."

"Oh, thank you," Nancy said gratefully, handing him the key. "If you find the trunk, please open it for me. The passport should be in the top tray."

"Describe the trunk."

"You can't possibly miss it," Nancy replied. "It is brass trimmed and has a tag bearing the number of my stateroom aboard the *Patrician*."

While awaiting the conductor's return, she and Ned wandered toward the lounge car. In the doorway the boy stopped short.

"Nancy," he said in a whisper, "Henry Washburn is on the train!"

He indicated a well dressed young man who sat reading a newspaper.

"Are you sure?" Nancy inquired in a low tone.

"Yes, I met him once at a party. I know I'm not mistaken. Would you like an introduction?"

"Not now," Nancy said hastily. "Perhaps later. Ned, he must be on his way to New York!"

"Probably."

"Perhaps he expects to sail on the *Patrician*. In that case, what a surprise Doris Trenton will receive!"

"You don't think she would like it?"

"She would be furious, Ned, and I can't blame her. It does look as if her father is scheming to throw the two of them together. No wonder she is rebellious."

Not wishing the young man to see them, Ned and Nancy returned to their own car. They did not have long to wait for the conductor, who came back in a few minutes and handed over the key.

"Oh, you didn't find the trunk?" Nancy inquired in disappointment.

"I found one trimmed in brass and marked with the initials N. D."

"That would be mine. My name is Nancy Drew."

The conductor smiled and shook his head. "I am satisfied the trunk isn't yours, young lady."

"But it *must* be mine," argued Nancy. "It was sent by express and has an identifying tag."

"This trunk has no express tag attached."

"But it answers the description perfectly. Brass-bound, and with my initials——"

"The key does not fit," the conductor told her with finality. "Except for the lock, some other person has a trunk exactly like yours."

Scarcely had the words been spoken when a terrific grinding of brakes sent the standing passengers sprawling in different directions. Nancy was flung with great violence against the wood paneling at the end of the car.

The railroad man was pitched into the entry-way, his head striking an iron rail. Though he groaned in pain, he arose and strove to calm the many travelers who were calling out from their berths.

The Drew girl wondered what could be the meaning of all this. Was it another jinx to postpone her trip?

She hoped not.

CHAPTER IX

A Diamond Bracelet

STRUGGLING to help herself and other passengers, Nancy Drew realized how many lives a locomotive engineer is responsible for in his daily run. Eager to learn the cause of the sudden stop, she and Ned went forward. They found that when a junction signal had failed and a collision had impended, the engineer had avoided a serious accident by his quick thinking.

Long after Nancy had retired to her berth she remained awake, reflecting upon many things; the near accident and the information the conductor had given her. If the key did not fit the trunk in the baggage car, then she could only agree with him that some other person had luggage similar to her own. Considering the queer circumstances surrounding her attempts to sail, she wondered if there could be any significance to the fact that a trunk like her own was heading in the same direction also. She determined to find out.

"I know what I'll do," she made up her mind. "When we get into New York I'll leave the train early and find out who owns that other brass-bound trunk."

In the morning Nancy and her chums were abroad long before the train crept into the station. But while they were among the first persons to alight, a disappointment awaited them. In vain they watched for the special piece of luggage to be removed from the baggage car. At last Nancy spoke to one of the trainmen about it.

"Oh, *that* trunk," he replied. "Sure, I know the one you mean. We put it off early this morning at Crestmont."

"Crestmont," repeated Bess, who stood near by. "Why, that's the town where Laurel Hall is located."

"So it is," Nancy agreed soberly. "The trunk may be owned by a girl from that place. How strange that it was put aboard the train at River Heights."

"How about a little breakfast?" suggested Ned hopefully.

"A *little* would hardly satisfy me," Bess laughed.

Nancy presented a claim check for Snowball, who had traveled in the baggage car, and gave the cage to Ned.

"I feel conspicuous carrying this animal," the young man complained as he led the way to the station lunch room. "Everyone is looking at me."

"Are you sure?" Nancy teased. "You know Snowball is very handsome."

Ned made a wry face as the young people

went to find a table in the crowded lunch room.

"Better not try to feed that cat in here or you'll start a riot," he warned as he saw Nancy gazing at her pet. "There's a time and a place for everything."

"Oh, all right," the girl said sweetly. "But the trainman may have forgotten to give Snowball her milk."

While the others studied the menu, Nancy glanced about the room. Observing Henry Washburn at the next table, she gave Ned a quick nudge.

"Why don't you invite him to join us?" she suggested.

Ned arose and went to the other table. After talking with the young man for a moment they both returned. As the introductions were made, Nancy regarded Henry Washburn with deep interest. He was well dressed, his manner was pleasant, and he was better looking than the average, yet something seemed to be lacking in his personality.

"No force," Nancy appraised him. "He seems like a weakling. I'll warrant he's under the thumb of Mr. Trenton."

When she invited the young man to join the group he accepted politely, sliding into the empty seat beside her. At first Nancy was careful to keep the conversation general, but before long she managed to mention Miss Trenton's name. Immediately young Washburn's face lighted up.

"Oh, you know Doris?" he asked. "I plan to surprise her by sailing on the *Patrician*."

"Indeed," said Nancy, pretending to be astonished.

"Her father and I fixed it up together," the young man went on. "Doris isn't to know anything about it until the boat sails."

"Your idea, I suppose," Nancy commented, drawing him on.

"No, Mr. Trenton suggested it first. However, I'll be glad to make the trip. Work never did agree with me," he added with a laugh.

"I should think it would be interesting to manage a large luggage concern," remarked George, studying him curiously.

"The novelty wears off pretty fast," he replied. "I own half of the firm, but I can't say that I manage it. Mr. Trenton handles all our weighty problems."

"I'll venture he does," Nancy thought to herself. Aloud she said, "Well, it will be nice traveling in South America. Doris should appreciate having you for a companion."

"She'll probably lecture me for leaving the business," Henry Washburn replied with a broad smile. "Doris is a wonderful girl but she has funny ideas. She thinks I should slave at a desk every minute."

"And you don't agree?" prompted Nancy.

"Oh, I believe in working now and then when I feel like it. But there's no sense in tying myself down when Mr. Trenton is willing to do all the worrying. As long as he is satisfied, Doris should be too. But she says she won't marry me unless I buckle down."

"You are in a predicament," Nancy said lightly. "Perhaps you should give in to Doris's wishes."

"And have her lead me around by my nose after we're married?" the young man chuckled. "Not much. I'll win her over to my way of thinking while we're on this trip."

When breakfast was finished, Nancy and her friends said good-bye to Henry Washburn, voicing rather outspoken opinions of him after he had gone. They all agreed that he was pleasant but lazy, unquestionably dominated by Mr. Trenton.

Nancy's first thought was to visit the express office, there to inquire for her trunk. She was told it had not arrived yet. A clerk assured her that it probably would reach the office some time that morning, but she could not feel easy in her mind.

"What will I do if it should be delayed?" she said anxiously to her friends. "Without a passport I'll never be allowed to sail on the *Patrician*. And this delay gives me so little time to find out about it."

Ned took the girls to the apartment of Bess's aunt, Mrs. Miller, establishing himself in a hotel not many blocks away. At once the young people were made to feel welcome, as they had been on other occasions.

"Any new mysteries since I last saw you, Nancy?" the woman inquired with a smile.

"She's trying to pick up a couple of them," replied George, "but we hope she won't get into a lot of trouble on this trip."

To take Nancy's mind from her troubles, Mrs. Miller suggested a shopping expedition.

"That's a splendid idea, Aunt Helen," Bess approved.

The girls did not buy many things but they enjoyed wandering about the great department stores. When it was time to return to the apartment house, they stopped at a jewelry store for a watch which Mrs. Miller had left for repairs several days before.

The shop was crowded with customers. While Bess and her aunt went to the repair department, Nancy and George sat down to wait. Almost at once their attention was drawn to a well-dressed woman with an expensive fur piece about her neck. She stood with her back toward them.

As the girls watched, she moved slightly so that they obtained a view of her face. She was Mrs. Joslin.

"We would run into *her* of all persons!" muttered George in disgust. "She must have come to New York to see darling Nestrelda off on the boat."

It would have been easy for the girls to have avoided meeting the woman, but Nancy arose and with mischievous intent sauntered to the jewelry counter. As she pretended to look at a tray of rings she noticed that Mrs. Joslin was examining a diamond bracelet.

"Haven't you anything better?" the woman asked the clerk.

"This is one of our finest bracelets, Madam," replied the man. "The work on it is very intricate."

"How do you do, Mrs. Joslin?" asked Nancy with exaggerated politeness.

As she heard her name spoken, the woman whirled about quickly. She looked not directly at Nancy but through her.

"I don't believe I know you," she said coldly.

"Why, don't you recall?" Nancy returned wickedly. "I am your detective friend."

"How dare you!" exclaimed Mrs. Joslin. "I —I never saw you before in my life!"

With an angry toss of her head the woman marched from the jewelry store.

"I hope I didn't cost you a sale," Nancy said to the man behind the counter.

"I doubt she would have bought anything," he replied, shrugging. "Nothing seemed to be good enough to suit her."

"This bracelet would please me," Nancy remarked, holding up the piece of jewelry so that it reflected light. "Is it valuable?"

"Nine hundred and eighty dollars," responded the clerk. "One of our nicest pieces."

Nancy called George's attention to the bracelet which was duly admired.

"Mrs. Joslin must have intended to buy it for Nestrelda," the latter said somewhat enviously. "Lucky girl."

"Anyway, she didn't get it," Nancy remarked. "How small of her not to recognize me. I wonder if she had any special reason for acting as she did?"

"She's a very silly, self-centered woman," said George feelingly. "The less I see of her the better I'll like it."

The arrival of Bess and Aunt Helen cut short the conversation. They too admired the diamond bracelet, then the party taxied back to the apartment house.

Although Nancy had tried not to speak of her troubles during the morning trip, she had worried constantly about the missing trunk. At the first opportunity she telephoned the express office to inquire if it had arrived. Her heart leaped as a clerk replied to her question.

"Yes, Miss Drew, the trunk came in at ten o'clock. You may examine it whenever you like."

After hanging up the receiver, Nancy cried:

"The trunk is here! I'm going straight over to look in it."

"And if the passport isn't there," Bess inquired quietly, "what will you do?"

A hopeful smile which had come over Nancy's face now faded from it. "It has to be there," she said grimly.

However, she again recalled the strange visit of the intruder who had sought to steal all her traveling clothes. There was great likelihood that he had taken the missing passport. Then what!

CHAPTER X

ACCUSATIONS

NANCY was very quiet during the ride to the express office. Even as she unlocked the brass bound trunk a great fear beset her that she might have had her journey to New York for no purpose.

George, Bess, and Aunt Helen crowded near, anxiously waiting. They peered over Nancy's shoulder as she raised the lid and burrowed down into the first layer of clothing.

"Not here," the girl reported with a sinking heart.

"Look in the lower part," urged Bess. "Effie may have put it down there."

Nancy raised the tray. There, on top of a neat pile of clothing lay several cruise circulars which had been left on the Drew desk. As she shook them, out fell the missing passport, together with other valuable papers which would be required abroad.

"Thank goodness!" laughed Nancy in delight. "I sail on the *Patrician* after all!"

Quickly she placed the papers in her purse and threw the worthless cruise folders into a nearby wastebasket.

"I actually feel weak all over," she declared, re-locking the trunk.

As everyone rejoiced that the passport had been found, Aunt Helen declared it called for a special celebration. She proposed that the young people be her guests that evening at a gala theatre and dinner party, a suggestion which the girls accepted quickly.

While Bess, her aunt, and George were a few doors away purchasing tickets, Nancy went to a telegraph office. Realizing that Hannah Gruen would not have an easy moment until she should learn that the passport had been found, she dispatched a message telling the good news.

Not until she had written out her telegram did Nancy pay any heed to the other persons in the office. As she turned to leave, a tall, thin man who looked strangely familiar, crossed the room ahead of her. A clerk called to him and he paused in the doorway.

"I am not sure of this word, sir. Is it *Imperio?*"

"That's right," answered the man impatiently. "And the name is Lopes." He went out the door and was lost in the crowd.

"I've seen that person before," Nancy told herself. "But where?"

Then suddenly she knew. He was the same man she had observed several days before in the company of Mrs. Joslin. Impulsively, without a good reason for her action, Nancy wrote down the two words she had heard the man mention. In reporting the conversation to Bess and George, she was subjected to considerable teasing.

"Oh, Nancy, you're always looking for clues," the latter laughed. "But I can't see what good these particular ones will ever do you."

"Neither can I," she admitted. "Still, one never knows what may develop. Often a scrap of information which appears valueless has been the means of bringing about the solution of a mystery."

"In this case, what mystery?" asked Bess skeptically.

"So far all I have is a hunch," Nancy admitted, smiling. "However, I can't help but feel that Mrs. Joslin is trying to hide something."

"Even if she does have a deep, dark secret, how are we ever to learn it?" demanded George in her usual, practical way. "Another twenty-four hours will see us aboard the *Patrician*."

"You haven't forgotten daughter Nestrelda, have you?" Nancy asked significantly. "She'll be traveling with us."

"On the same boat, you mean," corrected Bess with an injured sniff.

"Anyway, we may be able to learn something from her," Nancy went on thoughtfully. "That is, if Mama Joslin hasn't warned her to have nothing to do with us."

The girls knew that Nestrelda might try to

make their voyage an unpleasant one. For this evening, though, they dismissed all thought of what might lie ahead, and gave themselves up entirely to enjoyment. With Mrs. Miller and Ned they went early to the theatre. Although tickets had been purchased ahead of time, they were compelled to take two groups of seats, for the entire house had been sold out.

"This is one of the most popular shows in New York," Aunt Helen told the girls. "It's said one must be prepared for surprises."

A moment before the main lights went out, Bess, seated directly in front of Nancy on the aisle, called her chum's attention to two persons who were occupying a box.

"There are Mrs. Trenton and Henry Washburn," she whispered.

"But where is Doris?" returned Nancy, turning her head to gaze at the couple.

"I was wondering that myself."

At that moment the overhead lights went out so the girls had no further conversation. From the very first the audience was treated to a series of novelties. There were several amusing episodes, interrupted by shouts from the gallery; candy vendors created intentional disturbances in the aisles; theatre patrons, who in fact really were part of the show, arose to argue violently with the ushers. By one means or another the audience was kept in a constant state of uproar.

Suddenly all the lights went out. Almost at

Bess's elbow someone gave an unearthly shriek. The girl screamed in fright, as did several others near by.

Directly behind, Nancy and Ned enjoyed their friend's discomfiture, thinking it was all in fun. When the lights went on they were astonished to see that Bess's aisle seat was empty. The girl had disappeared.

"Where did she go?" Nancy whispered to George.

"I'm sure I don't know," the other answered. "She just screamed. Until the lights went on I thought she was sitting beside me."

As time went on and Bess did not return, Nancy became increasingly uneasy. Finally, unable to satisfy herself that all was well, she quietly left her seat and went to search for her chum.

Finding no trace of the girl in the lobby, she entered the powder room. It was deserted save for a colored maid, who insisted that no one had been there during the past fifteen minutes.

"I can't understand what became of Bess," Nancy thought nervously. "She wouldn't just get up and leave the theatre without a word of explanation. Something is wrong."

After wandering about the lobby again, she finally decided to return to her friends. As she entered the back part of the theatre, a ripple of handclapping came from the audience.

Glancing toward the stage, Nancy stopped

short and stared. Bess, looking very lovely in her white evening dress and silver slippers, was being presented with a five-dollar bill, her prize award for permitting herself to be "kidnaped."

"The joke is on me," Nancy told herself ruefully. "I might have guessed."

She tried to slip back to her seat, but Bess managed to reach the aisle ahead of her.

"That was one time you were fooled, Nancy," she chuckled, proudly displaying her award money. "Were you much worried?"

"I was beginning to be," Nancy admitted truthfully.

"Didn't you see the usher hand me a card when we took these aisle seats?"

Nancy shook her head.

"It explained what would happen and requested me to cooperate. I did, and now I am five dollars richer."

"They should have given you ten dollars for that scream," Ned chuckled appreciatively. "It was a honey!"

The show went on for some time, but after Bess's "kidnaping" the young people had lost their capacity for surprise. Following the entertainment, they all enjoyed a supper at a nearby hotel.

"Time we should be starting home," Aunt Helen declared at length. "Your parents won't thank me for keeping you out so late."

"Oh, this is an occasion," laughed Bess.

"There never will be another night like it. We're relaxing after Nancy frightened us by losing her passport."

"Tomorrow at this time I'll be aboard the *Patrician*," the Drew girl said softly. "I've always dreamed of sailing away to South America and now it is a reality. Still, I'll feel better when I'm actually on the ship and the gangplank has been lifted!"

A taxi dropped Ned at his hotel, then went on to Mrs. Miller's apartment house. As the girls paid the driver, they noticed another car standing near by but thought little about it. However, upon entering the building, two men stepped forward, blocking the way. A third, whom Nancy immediately recognized as the jewelry store clerk, hovered in the background.

"Those are the girls," he said tersely. "They are the ones who took the bracelet."

"Why, what is the meaning of this?" asked Bess's aunt.

The two men, still blocking the entrance to the elevator, opened their coats and displayed badges.

"You are plainclothesmen!" the woman gasped.

"These two girls are under arrest." One of the detectives took Nancy by the arm while his companion held George in a firm grasp.

"What have we done?" cried Nancy indignantly. "You have no right to arrest us."

"Either you or your friend stole a diamond bracelet from our store!" accused the jewelry clerk, stepping forward to face her. "I'm not positive which girl it was. That's for the police to learn."

CHAPTER XI

A Race with Time

NANCY AND GEORGE were aghast at the accusation which had been made against them. As they began to talk excitedly, protesting their innocence, Aunt Helen wisely urged the men to accompany her upstairs where the matter could be discussed in some privacy. When the apartment door had closed, she said quietly:

"Now tell us what this is all about. I am sure the girls did not steal a diamond bracelet."

"It is this way, Madam," declared the clerk. "A woman came into the shop to look at the bracelet. After she had gone, these two girls stepped up and examined it also. They said they would like to have one like it."

"You can't arrest us for that!" broke in George angrily. "I'd like to have an automobile too, but I don't intend to steal one."

"You and your friend were left alone with the bracelet at least ten minutes."

"Alone!" exclaimed Nancy, losing patience. "Why, there were dozens of other persons in the store."

"But not at my counter," stated the man confidently.

"How can you be sure if you weren't there yourself?" Nancy asked, and her remark caused the two plainclothesmen to nod in agreement.

"These girls stole the bracelet!" the clerk accused, turning to the detectives. "Aren't you going to take them to headquarters?"

"Let's not be too hasty," replied one of the men. "You gave us to understand you actually had seen them take the bracelet."

"False arrest is a very serious matter," Nancy interposed adroitly. "I know, because my father is a lawyer."

"Oh, a lawyer, eh?" replied one of the policemen, gazing significantly at his companion. "And what is his name?"

"Carson Drew."

Nancy scarcely hoped that her father would be known to these men, but she was elated to observe that the name meant something to the detectives.

"You're Carson Drew's daughter?" she was questioned.

"Yes, and I hardly think Dad would like it if I were arrested."

"I don't think he would either," was the grim response. "I have a feeling there might be trouble to pay, Jim. I guess we've made a mistake."

"That's the way I figure," responded his companion with a meaning look at the jewelry clerk. "There's no real evidence against these girls."

"But they must be guilty," argued the man from the store. "If I don't recover the bracelet I may have to pay for it out of my own salary."

"I am sorry about that," said Nancy. "Didn't you put the bracelet back in the case?"

"I—I don't remember. I meant to do it. Yes, I must have."

"Wouldn't it have been possible for someone to have removed the bracelet long after I had left the store?" Nancy asked significantly.

"Miss Drew, maybe you have an idea who made the snatch," spoke up one of the detectives as the clerk remained silent. "Did you notice anyone in the store who looked or acted suspiciously?"

"Possibly I did," returned Nancy, "but I have no real evidence. Without it I would be foolish to make an accusation."

"There have been too many false accusations already," declared Bess spiritedly, her eyes flashing.

After the detectives had left the apartment the three girls talked over their own theories regarding the theft. Bess and George were inclined to agree with Nancy that Mrs. Joslin might have had some connection with the robbery.

"She pretended not to know me, you remember," said Nancy reflectively. "And we saw Mrs. Joslin and that strange man at a jewelry store once before. Now isn't it possible that I frightened the woman away from the shop before she had an opportunity to take the brace-let?''

"Either she or that man may have returned later and stolen it!" cried Bess.

"But the Joslins are supposed to be persons of wealth and position," protested George. "It would be dreadful of us to make trouble for them unless we were positive."

"We can do nothing, of course," replied Nancy as she prepared for bed. "Theory and fact are far removed. But at least it's an interesting speculation."

Early the next morning the girls left Snowball in Aunt Helen's care and went to the steamship offices to make certain there had been no mix-up in assigning them new accommodations. As an afterthought Nancy asked if she might examine the passenger list.

"Looking for a friend?" George questioned her curiously.

"Not exactly. I thought I would see if Nestrelda Joslin's cabin will be in our section of the ship."

The girls examined the list carefully from A to Z. They were unable to find anyone by the name of Joslin.

"Perhaps Nestrelda isn't going after all," remarked George. "How nice that would be."

"Her mother is here in New York so she must be sailing," Nancy reminded her chums. "And Mrs. Joslin made such a fuss about everything."

Thinking that they might have skipped the name, Bess went over the list a second time.

"Look, Nancy!" She pointed to the name of N. Darlington. "Here is someone with your initials, N. D."

"It must be a man," supplied George, and she added with a laugh, "I hope he doesn't own a brass bound trunk."

"Not much chance of that," replied Bess. "The one which duplicated Nancy's was put off at Crestmont."

The girls did not tarry long at the steamship offices because they knew that Bess's aunt had planned a farewell party in their honor.

Returning to the apartment, they found the rooms beautifully decorated with flowers and everything in readiness for the gala occasion! A table had been set with gleaming glass and polished silver; there were tiny steamboats for place cards, each bearing a verse of poetry composed by Mrs. Miller.

At one o'clock Ned arrived, bringing with him two college friends, Albert Clark and Howard Brady. Greatly to his annoyance, the latter young man exchanged place cards and so managed to sit next to Nancy at the table. Before the luncheon ended it was evident that he had developed a deep liking for her. Everyone save Ned had a wonderful time, and the hostess felt well repaid for the work to which she had gone in planning the party.

The hours sped by swiftly. Soon it was time

for the young people to gather their luggage together and taxi to the wharf. Drawing near the waterfront, the cab was held up by heavy traffic.

As Nancy glanced out the window to see why they were being detained, her attention was drawn to a familiar figure in another cab directly opposite. It was traveling the other way, apparently having come from the dock.

The auto was occupied by a lone male passenger. As he turned his head toward her Nancy recognized the same red-haired young man whose car had struck her coupe in River Heights.

To the amazement of her friends, the girl rolled down the window and motioned for the other cab to stop. When it moved on siowly, she called to her own driver:

"Oh, please turn around! Follow that blue cab!"

"Nancy, have you lost your mind!" exclaimed Bess. "We're trying to catch a boat!"

"We have plenty of time. I want to stop that fellow before he gets away. I owe him fifty dollars."

The cab driver made an attempt to turn the car in the street, only to have a policeman shout:

"Hey, you, what do you think you're doing? Keep going!"

"Oh, that taxi will get away," Nancy moaned, looking back through the window.

"No, it won't," announced Howard Brady.
"Nothing like that will happen."

Telling the driver to stop, he seized Nancy
by the hand and pulled her from the cab. Then,
as the other young people stared, he signaled
another taxi traveling in the opposite direction
and bundled the Drew girl into it.

"A young man of action," observed Bess
dryly.

"Too much action," replied Ned, his face
darkening. "Like as not he'll make Nancy miss
her boat."

The cab bearing the two pursuers sped after
the blue taxi. Ten minutes later they both drew
up in front of a hotel in the downtown section
of the city.

"Your man went inside," informed the cab
driver as Howard Brady opened the car door
for Nancy.

"Wait here for us," the young man instructed.

Nancy did not know the name of the person
she sought and the desk clerk only shook his
head when she tried to describe the man. She
had far better luck when she talked with the
elevator boy.

"Sure, I took a red-haired fellow up not a
minute ago," he told her. "Twelfth floor. No,
I don't know his room number."

Nancy studied her wrist watch. Time was
passing swiftly and she must not risk missing

her boat. Still, it would take only a few minutes longer to investigate the twelfth floor.

The elevator shot upward with the couple but there was no sign of any person in the halls. Nancy and her friend walked hurriedly up and down, searching for the red-haired man. They knew that he must have gone into one of the rooms but they had no way of learning which one.

"If only a maid would come along I might gain information from her!" Nancy said in despair. "How disappointing!"

"I guess we've lost him," admitted Howard Brady. "We ought to get back now to the boat."

Nancy nodded and turned toward the elevator again. As she passed room 1245 she paused suddenly, for she had heard the sound of voices from within.

"Listen!" she commanded, as her companion also halted.

They could hear a woman crying. A girl with a quiet voice was trying to sooth her.

"Don't worry, Mother," she murmured, "everything will be all right. I'll be ready in a moment."

"But suppose your father had come!"

"He didn't, Mother, so why worry?" was the response. "Please don't cry any more."

Howard Brady started to move on, for the words meant nothing to him. He was startled when Nancy placed a detaining hand on his wrist.

"No, wait a moment," she whispered. "I am certain I've heard those voices before! I must learn who is in that room!"

CHAPTER XII

FAMILIAR VOICES

NANCY was not left in doubt long regarding the identity of the persons in the hotel room. A porter soon came down the hall and rapped on the door. As he was admitted, the Drew girl caught a glimpse of Mrs. Trenton sitting on the bed. Her daughter, Doris, indicated the handluggage which the boy was to take with him.

It occurred to Nancy that the red-haired man might be in the room also, so she waited. In a moment the porter came out with the luggage, followed by the two women. Mrs. Trenton drew in her breath as she saw Nancy, and barely inclined her head in token of recognition.

Doris avoided looking directly at Nancy. She responded to the greeting in a nervous manner. Without pausing to chat, the two women followed the porter down the hallway.

The room door had been left open. Nancy waited until Doris and her mother were out of sight, then looked inside. The room was in disorder but quite empty.

"No one here," the girl said in disappointment.

Howard Brady regarded her curiously. "Did you expect to find someone?"

"Well, I didn't know. Doris is acquainted with that red-haired man we were after."

"We seem to have lost him," the young fellow replied. "If you're expecting to catch your boat, I'm afraid we'll have to give up the chase."

"Yes, my friends will be worried, no doubt."

Nancy saw no sign of either Mrs. Trenton or her daughter in the hotel lobby. She and Howard went to their waiting taxi and a short time later drew up at the dock where the *Patrician* was being loaded.

"Thank goodness, you're back at last!" cried Bess, running to meet her chum. "You nearly gave us heart failure, running off the way you did."

"I knew I had plenty of time, so I took the chance."

"Maybe you did, but how were we to know?" demanded George, joining the group. "We've been worried sick for fear you would miss the boat. And all because you wished to give away fifty dollars!"

"I didn't succeed, at any rate," Nancy said ruefully. "We traced the man to a hotel but lost him."

"Let's get Nancy on the boat before she decides to go off on any other wild trips," spoke Ned a trifle crossly.

The girls showed their tickets and passports, then all the members of the party were permitted to board the *Patrician*. A steward led the way to an attractive cabin on A deck. He opened the windows to let in fresh air and unlocked the door to a connecting bath.

"Isn't this wonderful!" cried George.

"Our friends didn't forget us, either," said Bess, pointing to the table.

There were several letters, four boxes of candy, gorgeous flowers and other bon voyage gifts. Nancy's eyes became suspiciously moist as she read a telegram from her father.

"I'm glad he doesn't know how close I came to missing the boat," she thought. "From now on I'll look after my passport and never let it out of my sight."

Making up her mind that she would give all her papers to the purser for safe-keeping, the girl set forth to learn where he might be stationed. The *Patrician* was a large vessel containing a maze of corridors. Before she had gone far the girl was hopelessly lost, but she kept on walking, knowing that sooner or later she would reach an open deck.

Suddenly she met Mrs. Joslin face to face. They both paused.

"What are you doing here, Miss Drew?" the woman asked in a hard voice.

"Why, I am just waiting for the boat to sail," returned Nancy sweetly.

The woman frowned. "You told me you would withdraw from the trip! You deliberately lied to me."

"Oh, no, Mrs. Joslin. I told you I would withdraw from the Laurel Hall group, and I kept my promise. I did not tell you I would not sail. In fact, you gave me no chance to do so."

"I'll not have Nestrelda in your company! I'll take her off the ship this instant," the woman stormed.

"That's entirely up to you," said Nancy, unmoved. "I know I shall sail on this boat."

"You are an insolent, stubborn girl," Mrs. Joslin cried furiously.

Repeating that she would take her daughter off the boat, the woman hastened down the corridor.

"Nestrelda must be somewhere aboard the *Patrician*," Nancy reflected, "yet it's very odd her name did not appear on the passenger list."

After a moment she turned and followed Mrs. Joslin down the corridor, thinking that she might find out Nestrelda's room number. At the corner she halted, for ahead of her was the girl's mother, talking in an excited voice to the man Nancy had seen in her company in River Heights.

While she could not understand the words, Nancy shrewdly guessed that her own actions were the subject under discussion. It dawned upon her that the man really might be Mrs. Joslin's husband.

"They're certainly acting in a most peculiar manner," she reasoned. "Nestrelda can't be their only reason for not wishing me to make this trip."

Convinced now that something important was afoot, Nancy decided to do a little sleuthing First she would seek out the Laurel Hall girls and see what kind of a person Nestrelda was. She had little trouble locating their staterooms, so that several minutes elapsed before she found them.

"Maybe I ought to go back to my friends," she told herself. "The boat is due to sail very soon."

At that instant she was arrested by a commanding voice from Cabin 20.

"You will do as Mother says, Nestrelda!"

Mrs. Joslin!

"I—I can't," replied a girl's voice tearfully.

"Now don't carry on so," the woman said. "Your mother knows best."

"But I've planned on this cruise for over a year," the girl pleaded. "Your excuse doesn't seem a reasonable one to me. Please, let me go."

"No, darling."

"You're not being fair! You've no right to ask me to give up the trip!"

"Get your luggage together, Nestrelda."

Nancy did not hear the reply, for suddenly the door was flung open. A dark-haired, wild-eyed girl who could not have been more than seventeen ran into the hallway and disappeared down the corridor.

Before Nancy had time to hide, Mrs. Joslin stormed out of the cabin, intent upon pursuing her daughter. Seeing the Drew girl, she paused long enough to cry angrily:

"This is all *your* fault!"

Then she hastened after Nestrelda. Scarcely were the two out of sight when the steamship whistle blew a loud warning blast.

"All ashore," called a steward, passing down the hall. "All ashore."

"Mrs. Joslin will have to work fast if she hopes to get her daughter off the boat," Nancy chuckled, going to find her own friends.

Bess's aunt, Ned, and the other two college boys were preparing to leave the vessel. Regretfully goodbyes were said and greetings exchanged.

"Have a good time, Nancy," Ned said in parting. "Your father told me I was to remind you of something the very last thing."

"Remind me of what, Ned?"

"That you're to leave mysteries entirely alone on this trip!"

"And yet I'm supposed to have a good time?" the girl laughed.

"All ashore," called the steward once more. "Last call."

Ned and his friends hurried down the gang-plank, taking their positions near the edge of the dock where they could wave to the girls as the steamer sailed away. Nancy's attention was divided between waving to her friends and in watching the longshoremen lower the last of the trunks into the hold of the ship.

"There goes yours," remarked Bess, who stood beside her at the railing. "I'm glad it's aboard."

Unobserved by the girls, a tall dark man had been watching the loading. As he saw the brass bound trunk swing through the air, he gave a loud cry which caused Nancy to turn toward him.

"Why, that's Mrs. Joslin's friend!" she exclaimed. "Now what is the matter?"

The man was gesticulating wildly, pointing at the trunk, and trying to attract the attention of those who were lowering it. They paid no attention to him, going on methodically with their work. When the last of the luggage had been dropped into the hold, there came a loud blast from the ship's whistle.

"Now what did he try to tell those men about my trunk?" Nancy asked, deeply puzzled. "He acted as if he were attempting to claim it."

"You and your luggage troubles!" exclaimed George. "If you ever go to South America again I hope you take a knapsack."

"The Joslins should be getting off the boat unless they intend to sail," spoke up Bess.

"The men are ready to lift the gangplanks."

At that instant Mrs. Joslin came running. Her hat was pushed at an angle on her head and she seemed fairly beside herself with anxiety. Rudely she made her way through the throng, looking for her daughter.

"Nestrelda! Nestrelda!" she cried in a shrill voice. "Where are you? You must come off the boat with me!"

There was no answer. A steward stepped forward and took the woman by the arm.

"All ashore," he said sternly. "You're holding up the sailing."

"I can't go without my daughter," Mrs. Joslin answered, trying to break away. Again she began to call at the top of her lungs, "Nestrelda! Nestrelda!"

"Madam," said the attendant, pulling her toward the gangplank, "you must leave the boat at once."

"I won't!" was the woman's heated retort.

Mrs. Joslin was still protesting that she would not leave as she and her dark companion were being shoved forcibly down the gangplank. Then the passageway was lifted, and with the bands playing, confetti flying, streamers of paper stretching from dock to boat, the *Patrician* moved away majestically. Nancy and her chums waved to their friends until the vessel was too far out for them to recognize anyone.

"My, it was fun to see Mrs. Joslin pushed off the boat," chuckled George as the girls turned from the railing. "What do you think became of Nestrelda, Nancy?"

"She may be on the boat still."

"Do you believe she would dare defy her mother?" George questioned in astonishment. "I'm sure she must have gone ashore by herself."

"I think she is hiding!" whispered the Drew girl softly, "and didn't leave the ship. I'm more interested than ever in meeting her."

CHAPTER XIII

NESTRELDA'S REBELLION

UNTIL the vessel had passed the Statue of Liberty, the three girls remained on deck. After the sky-line of New York had faded into the horizon, they busied themselves making arrangements for deck chairs and a table in the dining salon.

As the girls wandered about, they met Senora Zola and a group of students from Laurel Hall. Nancy noticed that the headmistress appeared to be worried.

"I seem to be in a predicament," the woman confessed to Nancy's question. "Mrs. Joslin has caused me considerable trouble. After having insisted that you girls withdraw from the tour, she changed her mind at the very last minute and decided that Nestrelda should not go."

"It must be annoying," said Nancy, not disclosing that the information was known to her.

"The worst of it is, Nestrelda ran away and hid when her mother told her to leave the boat," the senora went on in her delightful rich voice with the attractive accent. "Mrs. Joslin ex-

pects me to find the girl and send her back with
the pilot when he leaves the vessel.''

"That is unreasonable of her.''

"I've looked everywhere, Nancy, and I can't
find her.'' She laughed ruefully. "Now, if I
had your famous detective ability——''

"If I see Nestrelda I'll tell her you are
searching for her,'' the girl said quickly.

She divined that the headmistress was on the
verge of requesting her to look for Nestrelda.
Nancy did not relish such an assignment, for
her sympathies were entirely with the girl. In
any event, she did not wish to be of assistance
to Mrs. Joslin who had abused her so shame-
fully.

"Thank you, Nancy,'' Senora Zola said gratefully. "I am going down to the cabins now to
see if Nestrelda has returned to her room.''

Separating from Bess and George, who
wished to unpack their clothing, Nancy walked
again around the deck. She paused to watch
two sailors with a trunk. They set it down on
deck, then started away.

Wondering if it might belong to Nestrelda,
Nancy went closer to inspect it. She stared in
astonishment as she saw that it bore her own
initials, N. D., and was trimmed in brass.

"There's something wrong about this!'' the
girl told herself.

Calling to the two seamen, she asked them
why the trunk had been brought up on deck.

"It's to be put off when the pilot leaves the ship, Miss," she was told. "The girl who owns it changed her mind about making the trip."

"But I am the owner," protested Nancy with some heat. "I haven't changed my mind, and I certainly don't wish to see my luggage sent ashore."

"Must be a mistake, then," conceded the sailor. "We may have lifted the wrong trunk."

"Whatever you do, don't put it ashore," Nancy said. "Please take it down to my cabin."

She gave the men the number and they promised to see that the order was carried out. Taking no chances, Nancy kept her eye upon the trunk until she saw it put into her sleeping quarters.

As she continued to wander about the boat, the girl kept watching for Nestrelda but did not see her. Neither could Senora Zola nor the officers to whom the headmistress appealed, find any trace of her. It came time for the pilot to leave the vessel and still the girl had not been located.

"What shall I do?" the woman from Laurel Hall asked Nancy. "The pilot refuses to wait longer. I can't even locate Nestrelda's trunk."

"She may have left the boat without being seen."

"Do you think so?" the headmistress asked hopefully.

Nancy did not really believe her own words so she answered truthfully:

"Nestrelda may be hiding aboard, but it seems to me you've done your duty. After all, since Mrs. Joslin changed her mind at the last minute, she is the one who is responsible."

"Yes, you are right, Nancy. I've done all I can."

After the pilot boat had motored away from the *Patrician* without its truant passenger, Senora Zola went to her cabin. Nancy, deciding to find out what had become of her pet cat, inquired the way to the place where the animals were kept. As she started down the companionway she came face to face with Henry Washburn.

"Hello, there," he said gaily, tipping his cap. "You haven't seen Doris, have you?"

"No, not since I came aboard. Are you sure she is on the boat?"

A look of consternation crossed the young man's face.

"She must be here! Her father assured me she would sail. I planned to surprise her."

"Well, I trust you're not the one to receive the surprise," Nancy laughed, and went on down the stairs.

She located the room where her pet was kept, and was glad to see such a well-ventilated place with an attendant in charge. She released Snowball from her confining cage.

"Hello, Puss," she said, allowing the fluffy animal to scamper across the floor.

Satisfied that Snowball would receive good treatment, Nancy left after a few minutes and decided to look around the third class section before returning to her own quarters. She had no thought of seeing anyone she knew in this section of the vessel, so was startled when she noticed a young man walking down the corridor ahead of her. His hair was light red in color and he moved with a familiar stride.

Instantly convinced that he was the person who had eluded her in the New York hotel, she quickened her pace. Hearing footsteps behind him, the man turned his head. Nancy caught only a fleeting glimpse of his face but she was sure of her identification. As if fearing detection, he pulled his hat low and moved swiftly down a bisecting hallway. When the girl reached the corridor no one was in sight.

"Now where did he go?" she asked herself irritably. "I believe he deliberately tried to avoid me again."

A stewardess came down the passage bearing a tray of food. Nancy Drew stopped her to ask if she had observed the red-haired traveler.

"Do you mean Mr. Smith?" questioned the woman. "He has red hair."

"And a moustache?"

"I'm not sure about that."

"Has Mr. Smith a room in this part of the boat?"

"Yes, the number is 572. Just around the next corner."

Nancy thanked the stewardess for the information. She waited until the young woman had gone on, then followed the passageway until she came to the designated room. The door of Number 572 was closed.

Nancy knocked loudly. Receiving no response, she tried again. At last she was satisfied that the occupant was not within at the moment.

"Oh, dear," she told herself. "I'm afraid he'll always try to avoid me. He probably thinks I mean to make trouble for him. Doris Trenton is back of this, I'm sure. I wish I could find out her reason for it. And I will, too!"

Nancy thought for a moment, then went down the hall to a writing desk which stood by the stairway. Taking pen and paper she carefully composed a note. It read:

"To the occupant of Room 572: If you have red hair, a moustache, and are the man whose car struck mine in River Heights, please communicate with me and receive fifty dollars due you."

She signed her name and room number and sealed the message into an envelope. Taking it down the hallway she waited until no one was within sight, then slipped it under the crack of the door.

"There, Mr. Smith," she remarked as she

finished, "I think that bait should snare you if anything will."

Suddenly, as she straightened up, all the lights in the corridor went out.

"I wonder what has happened," Nancy thought, as she tried to grope her way in the overwhelming darkness.

Then, without warning, a strange cold hand grasped hers.

CHAPTER XIV

NANCY'S MISTAKE

"WHO are you?" asked Nancy, pulling away from the person who had grasped her hand.

The stranger melted away in the darkness without replying. When the bright lights flickered on a few moments later, no one was in sight. The Drew girl was mystified. Had the current been shut off on purpose, or was it just a coincidence? Why had the unknown person acted so strangely?

Nancy walked about for a time thinking of the episode before returning to the cabin which she shared with Bess and George. The two girls had nearly finished unpacking during her absence, but the room was crowded with suitcases and trunks.

"How does one get in here anyway?" Nancy laughed from the doorway. "Trunks to the right of me, trunks to the left——"

"We'll soon have ours out of sight," declared Bess, shaking wrinkles from an evening dress.

"You should talk, Nancy Drew!" added George severely. "You'll find that extra trunk will be a nuisance when we get to South America."

"Extra trunk?"

George indicated a brass bound one which stood by the bed. "The other one is over there," she told her chum.

Nancy's gaze fell upon a second brass bound trunk which to all appearances was an exact duplicate of the first one. Both bore the initials "N. D." in brass.

"Well, if that isn't odd!" the girl exclaimed. "Someone has a trunk exactly like mine!"

"You mean one of these isn't yours?" queried Bess.

"No, I had only one. Which one of them is mine?"

As Nancy tried to find her key, Bess bent down to examine the tag of the trunk nearest at hand.

"This one says 'N. Darlington,'" she reported. "The steward must have brought it to the wrong cabin."

"I guess I was the person who made the mistake," confessed Nancy ruefully.

"You?"

"Yes, I saw two crew members with it and thought it was mine. I ordered it brought to my cabin. Otherwise it would have been put off when the pilot left the ship."

"Then the seamen originally mistook it for Nestrelda's trunk?" inquired George in bewilderment.

"I think they did. You see, Mrs. Joslin's friend gave some orders about the luggage. He pointed out this trunk to the men, for I saw him.''

"It's all a mix-up," said Bess with a shrug. "At any rate you saved the trunk for this man N. Darlington. He should be exceedingly grateful.''

"I'll explain at the office and have the trunk removed at once," decided Nancy. "Do you think I should apologize to Mr. Darlington too?''

"Why don't you write a note and slip it under a luggage strap?" suggested George. "It would save a lot of trouble.''

"That's a good idea. I'll do it.''

Nancy wrote a brief note to the unknown owner of the trunk. Fearing that it would be lost if she merely laid it beneath one of the leather straps, she looked about for a more secure place. Noticing that the ball-like brass trimmings were somewhat loose at the edges, she tried to slip the folded paper beneath them.

"No, I guess it won't work," she said aloud. "But I've learned something about this trunk, girls.''

"What?" inquired George with interest.

"It isn't exactly like mine after all.''

"In what way is it different? It looks just the same to me.''

"See those brass nails? They're twice as close together as those on my trunk.''

"Yes, they are, Nancy. I hadn't noticed them before.''

"At least if N. Darlington and I have another mix-up in luggage I'll be able to tell my own trunk," Nancy laughed. "Well, I'm on my way to the office now to report the matter."

Leaving her chums to finish unpacking, she hurried away. As she rounded a corner, the girl came unexpectedly upon Doris Trenton, who was sitting by herself in a deck chair looking at the sunset. Her face brightened as she saw Nancy.

"Why, hello," the young woman greeted her cordially. "It seems nice to see someone I know."

Recalling how distant Miss Trenton had been only a few hours before, Nancy wondered at the quick change of attitude. However, she wisely gave no sign that she thought anything might be amiss. Instead, she responded to the greeting and inquired casually:

"Have you seen many persons aboard whom you know?"

"Not a one, Miss Drew. The voyage promises to be a rather tiresome experience."

Nancy found it hard not to reveal that Henry Washburn was on the *Patrician,* but she decided that the young woman should learn the fact herself. Of one thing she was certain; the voyage would not prove boring for Miss Trenton, once she had learned the trick which had been played upon her.

Nancy might better have divulged the information, because at that very moment Henry

Washburn came striding down the deck. Smiling in delight, he walked straight toward Doris. The young woman half rose from her deck chair, stared blankly, then without a word fell in a faint.

"She's had a heart attack!" Washburn cried excitedly. "Call a doctor! Do something, quick!"

"You go for the doctor," instructed Nancy quietly. She did not believe that Doris had suffered a heart attack, but she thought it would be wise for the young man to be absent when the girl should revive.

While Henry Washburn hastened away to do her bidding, Nancy, aided by a stewardess and another passenger, carried Doris to her cabin. Under proper treatment the girl soon opened her eyes, to gaze about the room in a bewildered fashion.

"Is—is Mr. Washburn really aboard, or did I dream it?" she whispered to Nancy.

"Yes, he is on the *Patrician*," the girl told her. "He planned to surprise you."

Doris buried her face in her hands, turning toward the wall.

"Oh, this will ruin all my plans!"

Nancy waited, but the young woman had nothing more to say. Presently she requested that her mother be brought to the cabin. As the Drew girl went to find Mrs. Trenton, she met Henry Washburn returning with the ship's physician.

"How is Doris?" he inquired anxiously.

"Much better, though seeing you so unexpectedly seemed to shock her. If I were you, I wouldn't try to talk with her for a while."

"I don't understand why she wouldn't wish to see me," he returned in perplexity. "But I'll do as you suggest."

The doctor went alone to the cabin, while Henry fell into step with Nancy. Apparently being in need of a confidant, he began telling her his troubles.

"Sometimes I can't understand Doris at all," he said, frowning. "Do you think she really cares for me?"

"Oh, I would have no way of knowing that, Mr. Washburn."

"So often she tries to avoid me," the young man went on, half to himself. "Mr. Trenton says it is just her way, but I can't be sure. I've even thought——"

"Yes?" Nancy prompted as the man hesitated.

"This doesn't sound very nice to say, but I know you'll not repeat my words. I've wondered at times if Mr. Trenton may not be trying to engineer a marriage for purposes of business."

"Have you any cause for thinking so?" Nancy inquired alertly.

"No concrete reason. It's just that Trenton is always sending me away to various places.

He doesn't encourage me to take any interest in the business. Now Doris is just the opposite. She says she'll never marry me until I buckle down and work like a slave."

"A rather contradictory family, I should say."

"Contradictory is right! A fellow doesn't know where he stands. Before this trip is finished I hope to have an absolute understanding with Doris."

Henry Washburn would have talked on and on had not Nancy cut the conversation short. She did not like to accept his confidence, knowing that she would make use of any information he gave her.

After leaving the young man, Nancy found Mrs. Trenton and requested her to go to Doris's cabin. She next reported the trunk mix-up to the chief steward, then went to the lounge to write her father a letter. Eight double pages were required to tell all her adventures since leaving River Heights. Nancy ended her letter by saying, "Perhaps there are no mysteries in South America, but I have found a couple of promising ones aboard the *Patrician*."

"That ought to keep Dad in suspense for a while," she chuckled as she sealed the letter. "I wish I could see his face when he reads this."

Nancy had not forgotten Nestrelda's disappearance. After posting the letter in the ship's mail box, she sought Senora Zola in her cabin, intending to inquire if the missing girl had been found. In response to her light tap, the head-mistress opened the door.

"I came to inquire about Nestrelda," began Nancy, then stopped as she saw another person in the room.

"Oh, she is here now," replied the woman. "Do come in and meet her."

Nancy hesitated, uncertain of the reception which she might receive.

"Please come in," she was urged. "I have been telling Nestrelda about you."

The dark-haired girl who sat on the bed arose as Nancy entered the cabin. She had been cry-ing and her curly hair was in disarray. Even so she was strikingly pretty.

"Nestrelda, I should like you to meet Nancy Drew," the headmistress said by way of intro-duction. "There is no reason why you girls shouldn't be the best of friends."

"How do you do, Miss Joslin," Nancy re-sponded politely.

She did not offer her hand, but Nestrelda quickly extended her own. The girl smiled as she said in a soft-spoken drawl:

"Oh, please don't call me Miss Joslin. I pre-fer to be known by my father's name which was Darlington."

CHAPTER XV

A NEW FRIENDSHIP

THE name which Nestrelda had spoken so casually could not fail to startle Nancy.

"I don't understand," she murmured in astonishment. "Isn't Mrs. Joslin your mother?"

"Oh, yes," the girl explained willingly. "Mother married a second time and now her name is Joslin."

Nestrelda's tone made it clear that she had scant liking for her mother's husband. Nancy longed to question her, but refrained from doing so in Senora Zola's presence. However, she made up her mind she would extend the conversation at the first opportunity.

"I have a little confession to make," she told the girl. "Your trunk is in my cabin."

"Then it is still aboard! What a relief! I was certain my stepfather had managed to get it off the boat!"

Nancy told how she had mistaken the trunk for her own and had ordered it sent to her own cabin.

"It was a fortunate error for me," Nestrelda declared. "If that trunk had gone ashore I should have had no clothes for the trip."

"Then you are determined to go on?"

"I can't very well swim back now," Nestrelda said with a quick laugh. "And when I reach Buenos Aires I'll find some way to bring Mother around to my way of thinking. It was unreasonable of her to change her mind at the last minute."

"Nestrelda, you should do as your mother wishes," interposed the headmistress. "Now if you'll excuse me, I will go and send her a radiogram. She will be very worried until she learns you are safe."

Nestrelda made a wry grimace which the woman did not see. Senora Zola went out, leaving the two girls alone.

"Mother won't worry about me as much as the headmistress thinks," Nestrelda said after a moment. "She's changed a lot since she married again. I hate my stepfather!"

"What is he like?" inquired Nancy.

"He's really older than Mother but he looks years younger. That's because he is so vain about his appearance. He dresses expensively. I can't honestly say his clothes are loud but they lack good taste."

From the girl's description, Nancy was satisfied that the man she had seen with Mrs. Joslin undoubtedly was Nestrelda's stepfather.

"I'll run away before I'll return home," the student from Laurel Hall continued angrily. "Mother can't treat me like a child forever."

"Have you any money of your own?"

"A little. Mother will cable me more. She'll have to do it!"

"And if she refuses?"

"I don't know what I would do in that case. I just can't return to the United States so soon. Oh, Miss Drew, won't you help me if Mother makes trouble?"

"Your mother would be very angry if I were to interfere in any way."

"She's been most unjust," Nestrelda returned earnestly. "I don't know what made her turn against you as she did. I'm sure I would be thrilled to have your detective ability."

Nancy warmed to the words, but she did not allow her judgment to be swayed by praise. Without making a definite promise that she would try to help the girl, she managed to keep the conversation on a friendly basis. At her suggestion they went to arrange for Nestrelda's trunk to be brought to her cabin.

As Nancy watched the girl unpack her belongings she noticed a strange marking on the underside of the trunk lid, "A Trenton Trunk." Instantly it occurred to Nancy that the luggage might have been purchased from the firm of Trenton and Washburn.

"Did you buy your trunk in River Heights?" she inquired of Nestrelda. "It looks almost like mine."

"I really can't tell you. My stepfather bought it for me."

Dismissing the subject as of no consequence,

Nestrelda asked Nancy where she would stay in South America.

"My chums and I plan to spend most of the time with a Mrs. Purdy. She is staying on the outskirts of Buenos Aires."

Nestrelda straightened up from the trunk she was unpacking. "Mrs. Purdy? You don't mean Mrs. Albert Purdy?"

"Why yes, do you know her too?"

"Mrs. Purdy is Senora Zola's sister. My mother is their half sister. Mother has always lived in the United States."

"Oh, I didn't know," murmured Nancy.

She was greatly disturbed by this latest information, for she could foresee any number of complications which might arise. Presently, taking leave of her new friend, she went back to her own cabin. Bess and George listened excitedly as she told where she had been for the past hour.

"You're very charitable to have anything to do with that girl," said Bess flatly. "Especially after the way her mother acted."

"Nestrelda isn't a bit like Mrs. Joslin. You'll like her."

Bess and George helped Nancy to unpack her trunk. A bottle of perfume had been broken and several frocks were badly mussed.

"You must have been thinking about mysteries when you packed your things," George Fayne chided, holding up a wrinkled skirt.

"This will need to go to the ship's dry cleaning department."

Nancy nodded absently. She was occupied with inspecting the inside lid of her luggage.

"Now what are you looking for?" asked Bess.

"Only a name. Nestrelda's trunk has a trademark on it called 'A Trenton Trunk.' I thought mine might be marked similarly, but it isn't."

The next morning Nancy arranged to have her chums meet Nestrelda. Bess and George immediately forgot their prejudices, and before long were calling the girl Treldy and chatting with her as if they had been friends for many years. As they were drinking bouillon together on the sunny deck, Henry Washburn strolled toward the group. The young man looked so lonesome that Nancy invited him to join the party.

Nestrelda and Henry discovered many common interests. They seemed so absorbed in each other that Nancy, George and Bess soon excused themselves and went below to exercise Snowball.

"I don't see why Miss Drew can't have the cat in her cabin," Bess protested to the steward. "I saw another girl this morning with a police dog."

"That was Miss Brownley," replied the attendant. "Her case is quite different. She is blind and needs the dog to lead her."

"Oh, I didn't know that," murmured Bess.

During the afternoon the girls observed Miss Brownley taking a stroll with her trained dog. The intelligent animal walked in a straight line ahead of her, looking neither to the right nor to the left. Whenever he came to a step he would pause, so that the leash became loose in his mistress's hand, thus warning her of uneven footing ahead.

As the girls stood watching, the ship gave an unexpected lurch. Caught off balance, the blind girl staggered and would have fallen had not Nancy rushed forward to seize her by the arm.

"Oh, thank you," Miss Brownley said gratefully. "I seem to be very awkward today."

"I do not think so," Nancy replied. "May I help you to a chair?"

"Please. I have lost my bearings."

Nancy not only assisted the young woman, but sat down beside her on the sunny deck. Quickly recovering her composure, the young woman made no reference to her affliction. She talked cheerfully of many subjects, mentioning that she hoped to earn money by appearing in public entertainments.

"I play the piano," she said without affectation. "I do imitations, too. I have done occasional radio work."

Nancy found Miss Brownley charming, and admired the courageous way in which she faced the future. During the afternoon she mentioned the young woman to the *Patrician's* hostess.

"I am glad to hear about her talents," Nancy was told. "We will ask her to appear on a program we are planning."

As the days wore on, Nancy wondered about Doris Trenton. Since her surprise meeting with Washburn, the young woman had kept to her stateroom. Her mother said that the daughter was seasick, but Nancy had other ideas of what was wrong. She had felt sorry for Henry, but after she had seen him several times talking in interested fashion with Nestrelda, it occurred to her that they might be developing a special liking for each other.

"That would add new complications to the situation," she mused. "I wonder how Doris will take it if she should lose Henry's affection?"

Nancy had not ceased to wonder about the strange marking of Nestrelda's trunk. At the first opportunity she drew young Washburn into the conversation. Without revealing the purpose behind her questions, she inquired what trademark was used by his firm.

"All our trunks are marked 'Trenton and Washburn,'" he replied. "We have used that insignia ever since I can remember."

"Your trunks would never be marked with only the Trenton name?"

"Not to my knowledge. To make sure, I'll

look in the catalog. I have one in my room."

Henry got the booklet, and for half an hour he and Nancy pored over the listings. They could find no trunk advertised bearing any mark save that of "Trenton and Washburn."

"I was almost certain Nestrelda's trunk came from your factory," Nancy said in disappointment.

"Nestrelda?" The young man caught her up quickly.

Having made this slip of the tongue, Nancy was compelled to reveal that she and Mrs. Joslin's daughter owned trunks apparently purchased at the same place.

"I wish I could see them both," declared Henry, immediately interested. "I might identify them if they came from our firm."

Arrangements were made with Nestrelda, who seemed pleased to have an interest taken in her affairs. Henry Washburn examined first Nancy's trunk, then the one which resembled it so closely.

"Either of these pieces might have come from our factory," he admitted, perplexed, "but I can't understand why they do not bear our insignia."

Returning to her cabin, Nancy found Bess and George impatiently awaiting her arrival. They thrust a sealed envelope into her hand.

"What is this?" inquired Nancy.

"That's what we'd like to know," answered George. "It was shoved under our door about five minutes ago. We didn't dare open it because it was addressed to you."

"I have no idea who could have left it," Nancy said, tearing open the envelope.

A puzzled expression came over her face as she read aloud the contents. The fellow had written a message in verse form that he'd like to meet Nancy and receive fifty dollars.

"Well, what do you think of that!" interrupted Bess, peering over her chum's shoulder. "It doesn't make sense."

"It does to me," said Nancy in chagrin. "I am afraid it means that I may have offered to give fifty dollars to the wrong man!"

"Nancy, you dearly love to talk in riddles," scolded George, losing patience. "What is this all about anyway?"

"There's no mystery about it. I thought I had located the red-haired man I've been looking for, so I slipped a note under the door of his stateroom. It may be that the stewardess gave me the wrong room number, for it turns out this fellow has no moustache," she added, as she read on.

"Maybe he shaved it off," George suggested. "Nancy, has it ever occurred to you that this fellow you think is a friend of Doris and the one she may be planning to elope with, might be a criminal of some sort?"

"No, I haven't," replied Nancy. "How could you figure out such a thing?"

Feeling important, George gave her ideas.

"In the first place, the man may be a blackmailer. He knows something about Doris which she doesn't want either her parents or Henry Washburn to find out. So when he wants to borrow her car, she has to let him take it."

Bess looked at her cousin approvingly. "That sounds reasonable. Go on."

"If he found out Nancy has solved mysteries, of course he would try to avoid her. That's exactly what he has done."

"He has until now," objected Nancy. "This note says he wants to meet me."

"Only because he wants fifty dollars," went on George. "I've often read that money is the best bait there is to trap a criminal."

At this last remark Nancy became thoughtful. There *might* be something to George's theory. In any case, it would be best for the present if she neither answered the note nor appeared in third class herself.

"Girls," she said some time later, "will you do a little sleuthing for me?"

CHAPTER XVI

DOING A FAVOR

BESS AND GEORGE were eager to help Nancy, so they promptly agreed to try their luck at sleuthing. Their chum proposed they visit the third class quarters, strike up an acquaintance with the red-haired man, and by adroit questioning learn if he ever had been in River Heights.

Unfortunately, the two girls lacked their chum's cleverness. After absenting themselves nearly three hours they returned to report they had involved themselves in several humorous situations but had acquired very little information.

"Didn't you learn anything at all about the red-haired man?" Nancy asked, trying not to show her disappointment.

"*The* red-haired man!" exclaimed George. "There are at least three of them!"

"But the poet in room 572 is by far the nicest," Bess added gaily. "He seems in need of fifty dollars too, but I couldn't imagine him being a crook."

"I'm not giving money away just for the fun of it," announced Nancy. "Is he or is he not the right man?"

"We couldn't find out without divulging

everything," Bess replied regretfully. "He didn't seem inclined to talk about himself."

"Then I may have to keep the money. I surely don't want to give it to the wrong person."

"You'll never guess whom we saw while we were wandering about in third class," George remarked after a moment. "Doris Trenton!"

"What was she doing there?" Nancy inquired.

"She said she was looking for a former nurse who had taken care of her years ago. Both Bess and I noticed that she acted as if she felt guilty about something."

"Do you suppose she could be trying to avoid Henry Washburn?" Nancy asked reflectively.

"That's what Bess and I thought!"

"There is really no need for Miss Trenton to remain in hiding," said Nancy, smiling. "I doubt very much that Henry would bother her now."

"He's developing a great interest in Treldy, isn't he?" commented Bess.

"Yes, the affair is becoming more serious every hour. They swim together, dance together, and play deck games. I am wondering how it will all end."

Time passed very swiftly aboard ship. The three girls never having crossed the Equator, received the usual initiation. With other passengers they submitted to duckings and fun making. One day Bess admitted to Nancy

she had sampled many unusual delicacies between meals after the boat had stopped at Rio
de Janeiro, Brazil. It was not long after this
call that the girl had a severe case of seasick-
ness.

"I guess I was too eager to taste everything,"
she groaned to George, who tried to make her
cousin more comfortable as she twisted in her
bed.

"I feel sort of funny inside, myself," sym-
pathized her boyish chum. "It's remarkable
how Nancy can keep going so strong. She never
loses a minute as long as there's a mystery."

"It certainly is true. The trunk episode;
Doris Trenton's love affairs; the red-haired
stranger; and the unhappy Mrs. Joslin and her
daughter; all keep Nancy up and doing."

"Where is she now?" asked Bess, holding
her head between her hands, for the *Patrician*
was beginning to pitch violently in the rough
sea. A storm was descending with increased
force.

"Perhaps I should look for her," answered
the other girl from River Heights. "I believe
she is up in the wireless room learning the system."

Without announcing herself, Nancy burst
into the room. "Oh, girls!" she cried, "we've
received an S. O. S. Our boat is going to the
rescue of a lumber freighter. It's so exciting.
Please come on deck. The storm is beautiful!"

"Why Nancy," groaned Bess, "you're insane to be out in this weather. You might get washed overboard. Let the seamen do the outdoor work," she concluded, snuggling into a soft pillow.

"Dear me, you are a bunch of sissies. Come on up! You never will see a scene like this again," the Drew girl insisted.

"Well, I'll go up to the lounge," agreed George, "but I'll not guarantee sticking out on deck with you."

Nancy grabbed George's hand and pulled her out of the stateroom. Up the stairs the girls raced. Most of the passengers were unaware of the call for assistance from the lumber steamer, the *Rex*.

The wind whipped about the girls as they attempted to get on deck. More rain clouds were gathering.

"To the port side!" shouted an officer to the seamen. "Make ready the ropes!"

All was hustle and bustle. Nancy hurried along, narrowly escaping tripping over a rope. George was not so fortunate, for down she tumbled as the sea spray swept over her.

Frightened beyond belief, as she slid along the rain-covered deck toward the rail, George screamed that she was being washed overboard. Nancy grasped her chum, untangled the line from her sport shoe and helped her to a cabin door. Instantly the Fayne girl disappeared inside, leaving Nancy to watch the rescue alone.

"Heave to!" shouted the men.

Lifeboats were swung from their davits. Oars were snapped into position. The three dories, well-manned, skimmed through the tremendous seas.

Nancy, intent on the scene, failed to see a girl huddled in a sheltered corner, completely swathed in a raincoat and hat. Now, however, her gaze turned toward her. In her hand she held a cablegram, which the wind suddenly blew from her fingers. Quickly Nancy made a move to retrieve it.

The young woman cried out in alarm as the paper floated further from her, but the Drew girl caught the sheet as it lodged in the wire railing. Glancing up in the pouring rain, Nancy beheld Nestrelda Darlington with outstretched hands, ready to take the message.

Offering profuse thanks, the girl seized the cablegram and hastily retreated to the lounge, saying the weather was growing too frightful for her. She made no mention of what the message had contained. Nancy wondered if it could be from Mrs. Joslin, with instructions for her daughter's stay in Buenos Aires.

Suddenly the sinking *Rex* hove in sight. It was evident she was doomed for the bottom of the Atlantic Ocean! Strange shivers raced over Nancy as she saw the boat gradually submerging. She was glad the *Patrician* had weathered the gale so well.

In a short while the crew was transferred to the large ship. Nancy noticed how haggard and worn the sailors appeared to be. Many of them grunted in Spanish, German and English their dislike for the fate which had overtaken them. They hated to see their beloved lumber boat vanish to the depths.

"I know you'll miss her," said Nancy sympathetically to the stalwart captain, who still tried to hold his head high.

"She was my old companion and friend. Nigh onto thirty years we sailed together," he answered the girl. "I'll sure miss the *Rex*." There were tears in his eyes.

The evening before the *Patrician* was to reach port, Nancy and her chums assisted in an entertainment given by the passengers for the benefit of the seamen of the lost *Rex*. With the ship's orchestra providing a background of music, they executed an intricate tap dance which was well received.

Generous applause likewise was bestowed upon Miss Brownley when she had her trained police dog perform various tricks. As an encore, the blind woman played several selections on the piano and gave a reading.

Suddenly there rang out a cry.

"Fire! Fire!"

Startled, the audience became hushed, then en masse rose from their seats. At that moment the performer's voice called:

"Stay where you are! It's a false alarm!"

The sightless girl started to sing and all might have gone well had not a woman on deck begun to shriek. Knowing that the blind Miss Brownley could not assist further as the audience began to leave, Nancy cried out loudly:

"It's all part of the show. Please sit down!"

Then she rushed toward the door and grasped the woman who was still shouting that the ship was on fire.

"Please stop," pleaded Nancy. "Everything is all right. There's no fire. The performer is a ventriloquist and her announcement was part of the entertainment."

In a few seconds the passenger was calmed and became sorry that she had caused such a scene without being sure of what she was doing. As she left the deck, Nancy returned to the salon, where she was greeted by bobbing heads and silent hand claps which said, "Thanks to you, quick-witted girl."

Due to the late entertainment, Nancy and her chums overslept the next morning. On the other hand, Nestrelda Darlington had spent a sleepless night. She was plainly worried. The crumpled cablegram from her step-father attested to her upset mental condition. She longed to discuss her family troubles with someone, but felt too timid to do so.

"I wonder if I could ask Nancy Drew to help me," she thought at last. "I feel so alone. Senora Zola would never understand how I long for freedom. Maybe Nancy would—I'll try," she concluded as she gathered together her various personal belongings prior to landing.

By the time all the girls had finished breakfast, the *Patrician* was within sight of land. As Nancy stood by the railing, Nestrelda came over to talk with her.

"We'll be in soon now, won't we?"

"About twenty minutes, so the captain just told me," Nancy replied.

"I don't know what to do," the other said nervously. "What do you think I should do, Nancy?"

"I don't like to give advice, Treldy. Have you friends in Buenos Aires who could help you?"

"No one with whom I could stay. I guess I may as well go on with the Laurel Hall girls as I planned."

"Why don't you? That would seem wise to me."

"My step-father will be sure to inquire where my trunk has been sent."

"I see," nodded Nancy sympathetically. "And you don't wish to change your plans just to please your step-father."

Treldy's eyes flashed defiantly. "No, I don't. It was unreasonable of Mother to change her mind about this trip at the last minute. I'm sure it was Mr. Joslin's doings. Oh, Nancy, won't you help me?"

"I don't see what I can do."

"It's very simple." The girl spoke so eagerly that Nancy knew she had thought up the plan long before. "You could have my trunk sent to wherever you are going. I'll give you my address. Later you could have the trunk forwarded to me."

The Drew girl hesitated, but only for a moment. She felt very sorry for Treldy in her predicament. "Yes, give me the address. I'll do that."

"Oh, thank you," the other murmured gratefully. "I'll do you a big favor some day."

Within half an hour the passengers were ready to leave. There was a flurry of excitement as good-byes were said and stewards hurried back and forth with luggage. When the dock was sighted Nancy hung over the railing to find Mrs. Purdy. For several minutes she could not locate her. Then from out of a crowd of men and women who were waving and calling in Spanish to their friends on the boat there appeared the little lady.

"Mrs. Purdy!" cried Nancy, finally attracting the woman's attention. Other conversation was impossible for the moment.

At last Nancy and her chums crossed the gangplank and lined up for the customs. Their passports were inspected briefly and returned. Trunks had seals pasted on them after having been examined.

"There, we're through at last!" exclaimed Bess in relief. "Now to see South America!"

"It's going to be hard to get around when we can't understand the language," said George.

"That's true," agreed Bess, "but I've heard

all the hotels and big shops have English-speaking people in them."

"Come on," urged George. "We mustn't keep Mrs. Purdy waiting."

"Just a moment," said Nancy. "Miss Brownley seems to be having trouble."

The girls saw that a long line of persons was being held up as the blind woman talked earnestly with several officials. The three chums moved closer so that they might hear what was being said, and were dismayed to learn that Miss Brownley's right to enter South America was being questioned.

"But I'll not become a burden to anyone," the young woman was arguing. "I may be blind, but I am in no way helpless. My wonderful dog is very well trained and I have always earned my own living, and a very good one, too."

"Miss Brownley is a talented musician," interposed Nancy, who wished to help. "On board ship she was our most popular entertainer."

When Bess and George supported their chum, the officials held a quiet consultation. After some debate they stamped the blind woman's passport and permitted her to leave.

"You girls helped me out of a most difficult situation," the blind woman said gratefully. "If you hadn't spoken in my behalf, I know I should have been sent back to America."

Nancy and her chums assisted Miss Brownley,

to a taxi and expressed the hope they would meet her again. Then with Mrs. Purdy they drove off in another direction. The woman was delighted to see Snowball again, and hugged and petted the beautiful cat.

"I am so glad to have you here," she said over and over again.

One by one the girls exclaimed over the sights in the beautiful city, their companion all the while explaining first in English, then in a mixture of English and Spanish, what various places were.

"We better stop at a bank and change some of our United States money into native coins," suggested Nancy. "We'll need it."

After this was done, the group drove to a charming home on the outskirts of the city. The girls were intrigued by the low square pinkish colored building, in the center of which was an outdoor patio with a glimmering pool and vari-colored flowers.

"I'm going to love it here," Nancy exclaimed.

"This was our family home," said Mrs. Purdy. "It has been closed for some time, but I think you will find it comfortable."

"It is like a dream place," said George, not given usually to sentimental remarks.

"Manuela!" called Mrs. Purdy in a low voice.

A maid of striking beauty appeared. "Si, Senora?" she asked, her dark eyes sparkling.

Mrs. Purdy spoke rapidly in Spanish, then said to Nancy and her chums, "Manuela will take care of your wants while you are here. She speaks a little English. What she doesn't understand she can guess at!"

The girls were escorted to a large bedroom with old-fashioned furniture. The charmingly draped windows overlooked the patio on one side and a broad expanse of lawn on the other. At the far side of the latter were trees and a small sparkling river, which the girls were told emptied into the La Plata.

"This place has atmosphere, and I love it," declared Bess. "Did you ever see such gorgeous flowers?"

Late in the afternoon the girls went for a walk along the river. Returning, they found that the trunks, including Nestrelda's, had been delivered during their absence.

"I'll have Treldy's re-sent tomorrow," Nancy declared. "That should be long enough to wait."

"I hope you won't get into trouble because of your kindness," said George.

"As soon as that trunk is on its way my responsibilities will end," Nancy remarked in relief. "Now I'll explain something of the situation to Mrs. Purdy and ask her to get a *cartero* for me."

"A what?" asked George, her eyes wide.

"To you an expressman," laughed Nancy. "To anyone living in B. A., a *cartero!*"

The following morning the girls again went for a walk, this time along the highway. When they returned, they noticed a taxi standing in front of the villa.

"Mrs. Purdy appears to have other visitors from the city," observed Nancy.

As the chums drew closer, a man hurried from the entrance. Jumping into the cab, he drove away.

"Nancy!" exclaimed George. "That man looked for all the world like your red-haired friend!"

"He did at that!" cried Nancy, catching her chum by the hand. "Come on! At last we'll learn who he is."

CHAPTER XVII

INFORMATION

MRS. PURDY sat on the porch of the patio with Snowball curled in her lap. She glanced up as the girls ran toward her.

"Who was that man?" asked Nancy of Mrs. Purdy.

"What man, my dear?"

"The red-haired one who just left here in a taxi. We saw him as we came up the road."

"Oh." Mrs. Purdy smiled wisely. "That was Harold Sand, a friend from the States."

"I thought I knew him," said Nancy. "Did he once live in River Heights?"

"Not that I ever heard, my child. I doubt that you have met Harold. Perhaps you would like to know him?"

"Well, it might be worth while," Nancy agreed in too eager a tone.

"Harold is an attractive young man. However, I must warn you that he takes very little interest in girls."

Nancy knew that Mrs. Purdy assumed the girl had taken a fancy to young Sand. She could not disillusion her without explaining far too much, so she remained silent.

"Will the young man come here again?" inquired George after a moment.

"Oh, yes indeed. He will stay with us."

"In this house?" Nancy asked, scarcely able to believe her ears.

"Yes. Harold asked to live here while he is in Buenos Aires, so I have arranged that he have a room by himself on the opposite side of the patio from where we are. His only stipulation was that he must not be disturbed."

"By noise, you mean?" questioned George.

"He wishes to be left entirely alone, free to come and go as he pleases. He'll not eat with us."

Before Mrs. Purdy could tell the girls more about Harold Sand, a bell sounded. Presently Manuela crossed the enclosed garden to answer the summons. Suspecting from the conversation that the *cartero* had arrived, Bess offered to go to her bedroom to show the man which trunk to take.

Nancy called to her, "If that is the expressman, please tell him to take the trunk to that address on Alonzo Street. The number is on that slip of paper on the bureau."

Bess stared doubtfully at the two identical pieces of luggage. Finally she pointed out Treldy's trunk, gave him the address and with Manuela's help counted out the correct amount of money for his work.

With surprising ease the man raised the heavy trunk on his back and marched out the door. Suddenly the air was pierced by an unearthly yowl. Snowball, having escaped from Mrs. Purdy, somehow had managed to get under the fellow's feet. He stumbled, and in trying to regain his balance allowed the trunk to crash to the floor.

"Oh, dear," cried Bess, "maybe you've broken something inside."

The man let out a torrent of words, the meaning of which Bess could only guess at. Finally he heaved the trunk to his back again, muttered "Si, Senorita," and started off. Bess sighed with relief when she saw the trunk safely loaded into the truck. By this time Mrs. Purdy, Nancy and George had come to the front door.

"What was the matter with the *cartero?*" asked Mrs. Purdy in annoyance. "I thought the house was tumbling down."

After hearing an explanation Mrs. Purdy recaptured Snowball and went to her bedroom. Nancy, Bess and George lingered for a time in the patio discussing the news the woman had given them.

"With Harold Sand coming here to stay, I'll have a wonderful opportunity to learn all about him," declared Nancy enthusiastically. "Luck is certainly with me."

"Don't forget that the young man doesn't like girls," George reminded her mischievously.

Half an hour later the girls went to their bedroom. Nancy decided to finish unpacking, but stopped short as her key failed to open the trunk.

"Oh my goodness!" she exclaimed, staring at the brass lock.

"Now what is wrong?" asked Bess with misgiving.

"The man has taken the wrong trunk! Treldy's is still here and mine is gone!"

"Oh, the stupid fellow," moaned Bess as she saw the mistake which had been made. "I pointed out the other one to him. I should have watched him more closely when he took it."

"I must telephone Treldy at once!"

With Bess and George standing beside her, Nancy placed a call to the house on Alonzo Street where Nestrelda and the other Laurel Hall girls were staying. After a long wait the telephone finally was answered by a maid who had difficulty in understanding Nancy. Manuela was appealed to and got the information that no one was in the house.

"If Miss Darlington isn't there, give the maid this message," Nancy said at last. "When the man brings a trunk, tell him to return it to me."

"Let the man take away the trunk?" asked Manuela.

"Yes, tell him he made a mistake and took the wrong one. Have him return it to me."

The maid spoke rapidly in Spanish to the other servant, then hung up the receiver.

"Do you think you made her understand you?" asked Bess dubiously.

"Oh, si, si, Senorita," replied Manuela. Then giggling she added, "She talk like a parrot. Over and over she say, 'Let the man take away the trunk.'"

Throughout the day the girls waited anxiously for Nancy's trunk to be returned, but as dusk approached they began to fear that the orders had not been understood after all. Finally they got in touch with the expressman at his home. He had delivered the trunk to the address on Alonzo Street, he told them, but had received no message from anyone there. In the end Nancy was forced to be satisfied with the fellow's promise that he would return to the city for the luggage early the next morning.

"Such a mix-up," she sighed as the chums stood beside her. "Now I'll have to telephone Treldy again and explain."

"Why not drive into the city?" proposed Bess. "It would be easier than trying to make another telephone call."

Learning that dinner would not be served until eight o'clock, the girls summoned a taxi and drove to Alonzo Street. They were greeted warmly by Nestrelda, Senora Zola and other members of the Laurel Hall party who had just returned to the house after a day of sightseeing.

"The maid has been trying to tell me something about my trunk," Treldy said to Nancy.

"It seems that a man brought it here, but another man came and took it away."

"The trunk isn't here now?" gasped Nancy. "Oh, it must be!"

The girl shook her head. "I've questioned the maid twice. She insists a man drove up in a big car and asked for the Darlington trunk. He gave her a receipt for it and went off."

"A receipt?" Nancy repeated alertly. "Let's take a look at it."

"Unfortunately the maid can't remember where she put it. Can you imagine anyone being so stupid?"

"Yes," said Nancy grimly. "We tried to talk with her over the telephone earlier today. Didn't she even ask the man's name?"

"Apparently not. Perhaps you could learn more if you were to talk with her yourself."

Nancy's interview with the maid was not satisfactory. They had difficulty understanding each other, and the simple-minded girl could give the young detective almost no information. On one fact she was positive: that was, that the man who had taken the trunk was a fine Spanish gentleman, not an expressman. Moreover, he was not a person from the States.

"He gave me a *peso*," she concluded, indicating a very generous tip.

The girl could not recall what she had done with the receipt, nor could she provide any worth-while description of the stranger.

"More than likely the receipt would be worthless if we should find it," Nancy remarked to Nestrelda, convinced now that the trunk had been stolen. "Of course, the man wouldn't give his real name."

"I don't know what I'll do, for I have almost no clothes," the Darlington girl said disconsolately, not gleaning Nancy's thoughts as to the true state of affairs.

"I am the one to do the worrying, Treldy. That trunk happened to be mine."

"Yours?"

"Yes, the expressman made a mistake and brought my trunk here instead of the one he had been told to take."

"Then all your things are gone!"

"Half of them, at least, unless I can trace the trunk. What puzzles me is why it should be stolen."

"Don't you think it might be a mistake, Nancy?"

"I'm afraid not, Treldy."

"But why should anyone want to steal my trunk? It contained nothing of real value."

Nancy regarded the girl soberly. "You are quite sure of that?"

"Why, of course. My clothing wouldn't be worth very much to another person; certainly not to a man."

"I don't believe the thief was after your clothing, Treldy."

"What could he have wanted?"

Nancy had no answer to the question.

"Let's hope it was all a mistake," she replied evasively. "If the trunk isn't returned by morning our next move will be to notify the police."

CHAPTER XVIII

A Mysterious Guest

Morning brought no solution of the trunk mystery, so at Nancy's suggestion Senora Zola called police on the case. Members of the household were questioned to no avail. The officers regarded the matter as of slight consequence, and offered scant hope that the missing luggage ever would be recovered.

"One thing after another has gone wrong since this trip began," the headmistress complained to Nancy who, with her chums, had taxied to Alonzo Street with some of Nestrelda's clothing. It had been decided that owing to the recent upset, the girl's trunk should remain at the Purdy home. "If this keeps on much longer I'll be a nervous wreck," the woman complained.

"You have had a trying time," said Nancy sympathetically. "But don't worry about the trunk. It wasn't anyone's fault; certainly not yours."

"Nancy is being generous," spoke up Bess. "I am the one to blame. I should have been more watchful when the *cartero* took away the trunk."

154

"In that case Treldy would have lost all her clothing," replied 'he Drew girl. "I really prefer it this way. Only half of mine are gone."

While Nancy made light of the affair, she really was worried. Already she was running short of fresh clothing. George and Bess were glad to give her anything she needed, but she did not like to impose upon them. She hoped her trunk soon would be returned, yet reason told her that here was a mystery which would not be solved easily.

Whoever stole that trunk did it deliberately," she told herself. "The person thought he was getting Nestrelda's luggage. But even when the mistake is discovered, it's unlikely the trunk will be returned to me."

Making up her mind not to let her own diffi-culties dampen the pleasure of her chums, Nancy insisted upon a sightseeing tour. An enjoyable time was spent in a tour of the city, and by the end of a few hours the girls began to get the feel of the attractive place and pick up a few Spanish phrases. They wandered through various build-ings and museums, concluding their day with tea at a charming little restaurant.

"Are you girls dreadfully tired?" Nancy asked as they engaged a waiting taxi a little later.

"My feet hurt me," confessed George. "Otherwise I have plenty of pep. What do you suggest?"

"Nothing very exciting. I thought I'd like

to stop at Alonzo Street and talk with Treldy a few minutes."

"George and I have energy left for that," laughed Bess. "Oh, dear," she sighed, "I've eaten too much again. I'll never get thin in this country with its rich foods."

The girls found Nestrelda at home. To their surprise she seemed to have been waiting for them.

"I was afraid you might not get my message," she said, leading them into a room which she shared with another Laurel Hall girl.

"Message?" repeated Nancy. "We have received none. Of course, we've not been home all day."

"I sent word for you to come here as quickly as you could."

"Then you've recovered the trunk!" exclaimed Bess, her face brightening.

"No, but I may have a clue."

"What have you learned, Treldy?' inquired Nancy eagerly.

"This may have no connection with it, but I thought you would like to hear it. Tell me, Nancy, are you acquainted with a man named Harry Halifax?"

"No, I have never heard of such a person."

"He was here today to see me, and said he knows you."

"That's strange. I am certain I've never heard of anyone by that name, but he might be a friend of my father."

"I didn't know the man either," Nestrelda went on. "He claimed to be acquainted with my stepfather. He said he had heard I was here and thought he would call; yet it struck me he came here for one purpose, and that was to get your address, Nancy."

"Did you give it to him?"

"No. Somehow his manner made me suspicious, so I told him I would try to find out where you were staying. He agreed to come back here tomorrow afternoon."

"Good. You did just the right thing," praised Nancy warmly. "I should like to meet the man."

"Then why not come here tomorrow? He will arrive around two o'clock."

"I'll be here," promised Nancy. "Don't fail to keep him until I arrive."

Enroute home she discussed the situation with George and Bess. They were inclined to share her opinion that the man might have had something to do with the missing trunk.

"My name was on the stolen luggage," Nancy pointed out, "so by this time the thief has probably figured out that the other trunk is in my possession."

"You believe the man will try to make an exchange?" questioned Bess thoughtfully.

"He may. At least he'll attempt to learn if I have Nestrelda's trunk. Girls, I have an idea!"

"You're looking at us with a most speculative gleam in your eye," declared Bess mournfully.

"What would you like for us to do this time?"

"I'd like you to go with me to Alonzo Street tomorrow. Keep out of sight during the interview. Then, when Mr. Halifax leaves, shadow him."

"But we might get lost in Buenos Aires," protested George. "It's such a big city, and so few people seem to speak English!"

"We'll be glad to do it, Nancy," declared Bess instantly. "I was responsible for losing that trunk and the least I can do is help recover it."

Arriving at Mrs. Purdy's home just before dusk, the three girls went to their room to dress for dinner.

"It's my turn to have the tub first tonight," Nancy laughed, seizing a towel and making for the bathroom.

"Save us a little hot water," Bess called after her.

The ancient pipes clanked and groaned as Nancy began filling the tub. Fifteen minutes later the water could still be heard running full force.

"Nancy has forgotten!" complained George good-naturedly. "The tub must be ready to overflow."

Bess went to the door and rapped on it. "If you don't shut that thing off there won't be any water left in South America!"

The taps closed immediately.

"Si, Senorita," called Nancy in her best imitation of Manuela. "I was day dreaming and just forgot."

She hurried as fast as she could. Soon she was out of the bathroom, her hair a mass of bright ringlets from the steaming it had received.

"I'll be surprised if there's a drop of hot water left," George greeted her. "You must have gone to sleep in the tub, Nancy."

"I was watching someone through the window. I became so interested I forgot to turn off the tap."

"Mrs. Purdy, I suppose," said Bess indifferently.

"No, it was that young man, Harold Sand."

George stared at her chum in surprise. "Why, I haven't seen him since he moved in yesterday morning. He's kept out of our way."

"On purpose, it seems to me," added Nancy. "That's why I was especially interested."

"What was he doing?"

"Eating a lunch down by the river."

"It's queer he doesn't take his meals with the family," George remarked. "Mrs. Purdy tells me he stipulated he must always dine alone."

"As soon as I finish dressing I'm going down there and talk with him," announced Nancy, vigorously brushing her hair.

"Do you think that would be wise?" Bess asked significantly.

"Oh, I think so."

"You might accomplish nothing and only succeed in frightening him away."

"That's true," Nancy admitted reluctantly. "I've thought from the first that Harold Sand was avoiding me for a particular reason. It might be better to leave him entirely alone while I do a little investigating."

From the window the three girls could see the young man. As they watched, he picked up his lunch basket and walked along the river bank.

"He certainly is a mysterious character," remarked Bess. "Several times I've spoken to Mrs. Purdy about him, but she seems reluctant to tell me very much."

"I've noticed the same thing," nodded Nancy.

"It's as if she were trying to keep a secret from us. Could it be possible that she is shielding him?"

CHAPTER XIX

Word from Home

DINNER at the Purdy home was always a formal meal, requiring a full hour and a half. Nancy and her chums found it somewhat boring to spend so much time at the table, yet the conversation never failed to be stimulating. Upon this particular evening they deliberately tried to induce Mrs. Purdy to speak of Harold Sand. Scarcely had the topic been introduced when the doorbell rang. In a moment Manuela came into the dining room and handed an envelope to Nancy.

"A cablegram," said George. "Oh, dear, that must mean bad news from home."

Nancy shared her chums' uneasiness as she slit the envelope and read the message, but in a moment she relaxed again.

"It's from Dad," she told the group. "He's at River Heights again."

"I hope nothing is wrong," murmured Mrs. Purdy.

"Oh, no, but Dad makes a rather strange request. He wants me to send him Henry Washburn's address."

"Have you it?" asked George from across the table.

"No. I didn't ask him where he would stay, while in Buenos Aires."

"Mrs. Trenton and Doris might know," suggested Bess.

"Yes, but I'm uncertain where they are staying. They acted so queer when I asked them for their address, I didn't press the matter. Oh, dear, Dad wouldn't have cabled for the information if it wasn't important."

"What will you do?" inquired Mrs. Purdy anxiously.

"Nestrelda might possibly know."

"That's so!" cried Bess. "Henry Washburn paid her a great deal of attention on the boat. She'll surely know his address."

To journey back to the city that evening was out of the question. After some discussion the girls decided they would wait until the following afternoon before visiting Nestrelda. As Nancy expressed it, she then would be able to kill two birds with one stone, since the interview with Mr. Halifax had been set for two o'clock. In her cable to her father she could ask him about the man.

The girls arose late, and enjoyed a substantial breakfast. No other members of the household were about, so they had the dining room to themselves.

"Have you seen Mr. Sand this morning?" Nancy questioned Manuela who came to take the dishes to the kitchen.

"Senor Sand—he went early to the city in a taxi."

Nancy was disappointed at the information, for she had hoped to find a means of becoming acquainted with the elusive young man. However, she was convinced that Doris Trenton had not eloped with him yet. The morning passed quickly, and immediately after luncheon the girls set off for Alonzo Street.

"What is it you wish George and me to do?" asked Bess as the taxi drew near the house where Nestrelda was staying.

"Just remain in the cab. When Mr. Halifax leaves the building drive after him. Learn where he goes and report to me."

"That shouldn't be a hard assignment," said George. "I hope the man doesn't keep us waiting long."

Scarcely had Nancy disappeared inside the hotel when Harry Halifax arrived. He was a dapper man of fifty with iron gray hair. His immaculate clothes were of the latest cut and he swung a cane jauntily.

Nestrelda and Nancy were waiting for him in the parlor. If the man were dismayed to see the Drew girl, he did not show it. Instead, as he was introduced, he bowed low and held Nancy's hand somewhat longer than was necessary.

"I would have known you anywhere," he said, cocking his head sideways the better to look at her. "You are the very picture of your father."

"Do you know him well?" Nancy asked quickly.

"You mean your father never spoke of me to you?"

"Not that I recall, Mr. Halifax."

"He has often mentioned you, Nancy. When I last was in the States, which would be nearly twelve years ago, you were only a little girl. You had the prettiest hair I've ever seen and you wore it tied with a pink ribbon!"

"I can't remember that far back," Nancy smiled. "Were you a client of my father?"

"Not exactly, my dear. I helped him with a case which involved a South American firm. Now and then when your father requires special information he writes to me."

"I see," said Nancy, feeling mortified to think she had doubted the man's honesty.

"You will give me your address?" Mr. Halifax asked, taking out his notebook. "I should like to keep in touch with you while you are in Buenos Aires. My wife no doubt will invite you to our home to dinner."

Nancy could not refuse such a reasonable request without appearing to be rude. Accordingly she wrote down Mrs. Purdy's address, then he left the hotel.

From the window Nancy saw him enter a taxi. She tried to signal to Bess and George that there was no need for them to follow, but they did not see her. The second vehicle sped in pursuit of the one in which Mr. Halifax was riding.

"Perhaps it's just as well they do check up on him," thought Nancy. "His story sounded convincing enough, yet I know Dad never mentioned a Mr. Halifax to me."

Now that the man had gone, she realized that his personality had influenced her. Actually he had given her no information about himself.

"Was I too careful, Nancy?" inquired Nestrelda a moment later. "I suppose I should have told Mr. Halifax where you live."

"I wanted to meet him, Treldy. You weren't a bit too cautious. Oh, by the way, have you Henry Washburn's address?"

Nestrelda's pretty face clouded. "No, I haven't. I thought he surely would telephone me before this. I gave him my address but I didn't ask for his."

"Then you have no idea where he might be staying?"

"He mentioned several places. Let me see, he might have gone to the Hotel Nacional. He spoke of that place."

"It's vitally important that I reach him," Nancy said, explaining about the cablegram she had received from her father.

"I don't know why Henry hasn't tried to get in touch with me," Treldy said unhappily. "He was so attentive on board ship. I—I thought he might be falling in love with me."

Nancy spared the girl the pain of learning

that the man she admired was supposed to be engaged to someone else. Instead, she changed the subject by asking her if she had heard from her mother.

"Not a word," answered Treldy, turning away.

While Nancy did not approve of the way the girl had acted, she thought that Mrs. Joslin had only herself to blame. Yet she could not understand why the woman had not tried to contact her daughter after she had left the boat.

"I believe I'll taxi over to the Hotel Nacional," she told Nestrelda as she turned to leave. "Would you like to go with me?"

"Why yes," the other accepted eagerly, "if I can be of any help in locating Henry Washburn."

Nancy was not deceived. She understood perfectly that the girl longed to see the young man again. As it developed, the searchers were doomed to disappointment, for although they taxied from one hotel to another, they could not locate him.

At length Nancy ordered the driver to return to Nestrelda's home. They were traveling down a narrow side street when the cabman suddenly slammed on the brakes. Peering out the window, the girls saw that he had stopped to avoid striking a woman who stood in the middle of the road.

"Go on!" shouted the driver wrathfully in Spanish.

The young woman moved uncertainly, turning into the path of a car which was coming
from the opposite direction.

"Miss Brownley!" cried Nancy, horrified.

Swinging open the taxi door, she darted to
the confused blind person and seized her by the
arm. "I'm Nancy Drew," she said, guiding her
toward the cab.

Miss Brownley sobbed in relief. "I've lost
my dog somewhere," she told the girl. "Those
street urchins unfastened his leash and took
him away from me."

"I'll find him for you," said Nancy grimly.
"Please step into this taxi where you will be
safe with a friend of mine."

She helped the young woman in, then looked
about for the missing dog. The urchins, observing the result of their mischief, had darted into
a nearby alley. The police dog, angered by the
treatment his mistress had received, longed to
take up the pursuit. Instead, being well
trained, he tried to locate the blind woman.

At the risk of being attacked, Nancy seized
the leash. The dog, remembering her as a
friend, allowed her to lead him to the taxi.

"I'll be glad to take you where you live,"
the Drew girl said to Miss Brownley.

"You are very kind, but I don't like to cause
you so much trouble."

"No trouble at all. Treldy and I have plenty
of time."

"I don't know what I should have done if

you hadn't rescued me," the sightless girl declared as the cab sped over the pavement. "I might have been killed. Those boys did not mean to be so cruel, I'm sure. They may not have realized that I am blind."

"I hope they are thoroughly ashamed of themselves," said Nestrelda feelingly.

"Have you found work since reaching B. A., Miss Brownley?" Nancy presently inquired.

"Yes, I am to have a part in a show which opens here next week. If my act is a success I'll have no difficulty in getting along from now on."

Nancy was relieved to learn of the young woman's good fortune. In parting she wished her the best of luck, promising to attend the opening of the show if she were still in Buenos Aires.

At Alonzo Street, Nancy bade good-bye to Nestrelda and motored alone to Mrs. Purdy's home. Bess and George had not arrived yet.

"I hope they didn't run into any trouble," Nancy thought anxiously. "The more I consider it, the more inclined I am to think that Mr. Halifax will bear watching. I shouldn't be surprised if he's trying to get his hands on Treldy's trunk!"

As she dismissed the cab and ran up the walk, Mrs. Purdy opened the door of the house.

"Oh, Nancy, I am so glad you are back!" the lady exclaimed.

"Is anything wrong, Mrs. Purdy? Bess and George——?"

"No, but a young man came here not twenty minutes ago. He said you had telephoned that you wanted your brass-bound trunk repaired."

"You didn't allow him to take it away?" Nancy gasped.

"Manuela was just going to let him carry it off when I interfered. I didn't like the appearance of the fellow."

"It was a ruse to get the trunk away from me," Nancy declared with conviction. "You saved the day, Mrs. Purdy!"

"I was afraid afterwards that I might have made a mistake."

"You certainly didn't. I wonder who the person could have been?"

"He looked like an ordinary repairman to me, but he talked very glibly. That was what made me suspicious of him."

"An agent for another person, no doubt," Nancy said, frowning. "Maybe Mr. Halifax sent him," she mused.

"Mr. Halifax?"

"He's no one you know, Mrs. Purdy. I met the man for the first time today and gave him my address."

"Oh, Nancy, was that wise?"

"Apparently it wasn't, but at the moment he seemed like a very pleasant gentleman, who insisted he knows my father."

"All this trouble you've been having over your trunk worries me," confessed Mrs. Purdy. "I think you should return Miss Darlington's luggage before something happens. I have such an uneasy feeling—I can't explain it."

"I hope to clear up everything in a day or so, Mrs. Purdy. Just as soon as I learn about Mr. Halifax——"

Nancy broke off speaking, for a taxi had drawn up to the door. Bess and George leaped out and hurried toward their chum.

"They're here now!" cried Nancy. "From the way they act, I'm sure they have news for me!"

CHAPTER XX

SCATTERED CLUES

BESS AND GEORGE could not control their excitement as they related their adventures since taking leave of Nancy at Nestrelda's home.

"We followed Mr. Halifax just as you told us to do," Bess revealed, speaking rapidly. "First he stopped at a store to telephone, but we weren't able to hear the conversation. Then he drove on to the offices of Halifax and Lopes."

"How was the last name spelled?" asked Nancy eagerly.

"L-O-P-E-S. This is the part that will surprise you, Nancy. They're manufacturers of luggage!"

"That doesn't astonish me at all," smiled Nancy. "What else did you learn?"

"George and I decided to try to find out if your missing trunk was there. We knew Mr. Halifax wouldn't recognize us, so we went in and pretended we wished to buy something. I think we examined every trunk in the place!"

"And yours wasn't there, Nancy," added George regretfully.

"We didn't even see one which remotely resembled it," added Bess.

"Did the shop have a repair department?" asked the cousins' chum.

Bess glanced at Nancy in surprise. "Why, yes, I believe it did. We didn't go back there, however."

"Then you missed the most likely place. I have a hunch my trunk may be there. Tomorrow I'll find out!"

Nancy went on to explain that during her chums' absence a repairman had attempted to carry away Nestrelda's trunk.

"It's queer why that piece of luggage is in such demand," commented Bess. "I simply can't figure it out."

Nancy had a hunch, so while waiting for dinner, the girls made a thorough examination of the mysterious brass bound trunk. They emptied the various trays and turned them upside down. They tapped the bottom and the sides for secret compartments.

"I can't for the life of me see why anyone would want this trunk," Nancy said, rocking back on her heels. "Yet there must be a reason."

"Nothing is hidden in it," added Bess wearily. "We've gone over every inch of it, I'm sure."

"Girls, you recall this same trunk was put off at Crestmont," Nancy went on.

"It might not have been the same one," interposed George.

"I believe it was. Now that leads to an interesting possibility. If the Joslins had possession of it for an entire day——"

Nancy did not finish. Instead, she sprang to her feet and ran to phone to Nestrelda. A few minutes later, her face flushed with triumph, she returned to report to her chums.

"I've just been talking with Treldy," she explained. "She told me that her mother gave her the new brass bound trunk just before she sailed from New York. It was supposed to be a gift from her stepfather as well. He insisted that she use it even though all her belongings already had been packed in an old trunk."

"Strange they couldn't have given her the new one ahead of time," commented George.

"That's my point exactly," declared Nancy, her eyes sparkling. "Mr. Joslin kept the luggage until the very last minute because he must have hidden something in it!"

"But we've looked everywhere," protested Bess.

"I know. The trunk seems to be empty."

"Has Treldy any suspicion of what may be wrong?" questioned George after several moments of silence.

"I am sure she doesn't. She told me over the phone that Senora Zola is greatly upset about everything that has happened. She plans to take the Laurel Hall girls to Rosario tomorrow."

174 Mystery of Brass Bound Trunk

"And will Treldy leave too?" asked Bess.

"Yes, she promised to send me her address as soon as she arrives there. I don't know what she expects to do about this trunk. She didn't mention it, so I didn't offer to send it."

Leaving her chums to chat with Mrs. Purdy, Nancy went to her bedroom. As she looked toward the river, she noticed Harold Sand seated on a bench not far away. It was the first time that the girl had obtained a really close view of the young man and she made the most of her opportunity to do so now.

"I keep feeling I've seen him in an entirely different rôle," she told herself, "yet he must be a stranger to me. I couldn't have met him before that day in River Heights when he struck my car."

Bess's camera, which the girls had used on their sightseeing tour, lay on the dresser. Obeying a sudden, irresistible impulse, Nancy picked it up and stole outside. Keeping shielded by bushes, she crept forward until she was within a few feet of the young man. Focusing the camera upon him, she snapped a picture and quickly retreated.

"He didn't even see me," she told herself as she replaced the camera on the dresser. "Won't Bess be surprised when she discovers an extra picture on the roll!"

Two hours remained before dinner would be served. Nancy's next move was to suggest to Bess that they take the films to a nearby shop which promised to develop pictures "while you wait."

Immediately falling in with the suggestion, Bess and George made the trip. In a short time the film was ready. Nancy let her chums look at the pictures first.

"Oh, this one of a cathedral came out grand!" exclaimed Bess in delight.

"This picture of me standing by the statue is awful!" declared George. "I'm going to tear it up!"

"What is this?" demanded Bess as she came to the one Nancy had snapped. "I can't recall having taken it."

"Neither can I," said George, peering over her cousin's shoulder. "Why, it looks like that young man, Harold Sand! Nancy, is this some of your work?"

"Maybe."

"Nancy Drew, we might have guessed why you were so eager to have the pictures developed!" cried Bess, laughing at the joke which had been played. "Why did you take the snapshot?"

"I can't really say. It was just an impulse, but I'm glad I did it. The picture may be useful later."

"You can frame it and keep it on your dresser," teased George, as the three started for home.

Nancy smiled as she studied the picture of Harold Sand.

"Notice anything about this pose?" she asked presently.

"Why, no," answered George and Bess together.

"I think I do," replied Nancy mysteriously. "The hands——"

She did not tell her chums what she thought, for just then they arrived at the Purdy home and were told by Manuela that a young man was waiting for them in the patio.

"He looks like Henry Washburn!" Nancy whispered, quickening her step. "Just the person I want to see!"

While on board the *Patrician* she had given her address to the traveler, little dreaming that he ever would visit her. After greetings were exchanged, Nancy showed Henry the cablegram which she had received from her father.

"I can't imagine why Mr. Drew would want to get in touch with me," the young man said in bewilderment.

"Neither can I," replied Nancy, "unless it concerns your business dealings with the luggage firm."

"But Mr. Trenton looks after our contracts. I have nothing to do with them."

"Anyway, it's important for you to contact my father," insisted Nancy, refolding the cablegram. "Will you send him a message tonight?"

"I'll do better than that. I'll get in touch with him at once by telephone."

"Oh, that would be fine!" approved Nancy. "You can make the call from here."

While waiting for connections to be estab. lished, the young people hovered near the in. strument. Gradually it became apparent to Nancy that Henry Washburn wished to speak with her alone, so she made an excuse for drawing him into the garden.

"I suppose you wonder why I came here tonight," he said hurriedly after the door had closed behind them. "The truth is, I need your advice."

"I'm always glad to give that," laughed Nancy, "though I can't say how good it is."

"I—I hardly know how to begin," he said self-consciously. "You are a good friend of Nestrelda, aren't you?"

"I like her very much," said Nancy care. fully.

"So do I. Until I met her I was sure I wanted to marry Doris, but now I don't know. Treldy swept me off my feet—she is such a tempestuous, lovely girl."

Nancy smiled at the contradiction of terms and waited for him to go on.

"Do you think it would upset everything if I should tell Mr. Trenton I cannot marry Doris?"

Nancy answered frankly, "It would cause difficulties of one kind or another. I am confident of that."

"But a man has a right to marry the girl he loves!"

"Indeed he has. But are you sure that Treldy is the girl for you? It might be only a passing fancy, you know."

"I hardly think so," the young man responded soberly. "My feeling is very sincere."

"If I were you I would do nothing for a few days," Nancy advised him. "Give yourself time to think over the problem very carefully."

Before she could continue, Bess came to the door, crying excitedly that the long distance call had been put through. Henry Washburn hastened to the telephone.

Nancy stood close by as the young man talked with Mr. Drew. She gained no inkling of the conversation, for Henry's comments were confined to "yes" or "no," and a few meaningless remarks. However, she noticed how pale his face had become, and his expression grew increasingly grave. At last he handed the phone to the girl so that she might say a few words to her father.

"Hello, Dad," she said, and was thrilled as his voice came back to her clearly.

"Having a nice time?" he inquired as casually as if he were talking across a room instead of an ocean.

"Wonderful, Dad. I met a friend of yours today, a Mr. Harry Halifax."

"Never heard of him, Nancy."

"You're positive he was never associated with you in any dealings?"

"Of course. Nancy, here's a bit of news which may interest you. Mrs. Joslin was caught in Boston yesterday for stealing a diamond necklace."

"She's been arrested?"

"No, she convinced the jewelers it was a mistake. They let her go!"

"A mistake!" cried Nancy indignantly. "Why, almost the same thing happened in New York. I could tell you——"

"Not over such an expensive telephone," interrupted her father with an amused chuckle. "Sorry to say good-bye, but tolls mount. Take care of yourself, my dear."

CHAPTER XXI

A Summons Home

Nancy hung up the receiver and gazed questioningly at Henry Washburn. The young man had slumped into a chair, the picture of despondency.

"Did my father have bad news for you?" she asked him kindly.

"He wants me to return to the States on the first boat."

"Oh! That upsets your plans, doesn't it?"

"Rather."

"Will you go?"

"I told him I would. Mr. Drew has been going over the estate papers and has found several things he doesn't like. He thinks I should come back and consult with him."

"I am sure Dad wouldn't summon you if it weren't vitally important."

"I realize that," admitted the young man gloomily. "The trouble is that if I leave now I'll not see Treldy again. And I had hoped— well, you understand."

For a moment Nancy had forgotten this angle of things. Since hearing her father's message, she felt that she should do everything to discourage the friendship. Later Treldy would take care of the matter herself. Poor Treldy! Things were piling up pretty heavily against her.

"She may soon be returning home herself, so your separation should not be a long one," Nancy said aloud.

"We *could* be married before I leave," the young man replied, struck by a sudden idea. "That is, if Treldy is willing."

Nancy was in a panic and countered for time.

"Do you think a marriage would be wise, considering the estate difficulties which may face you?" she asked.

"I suppose it would be a foolish thing to do," Henry acknowledged gloomily.

Nancy's private opinion was that the young man had been saved by circumstance from a very rash act. She believed, too, that his feeling for Nestrelda was nothing more than infatuation.

"I'll just talk with Treldy on the phone before I sail," he said finally. "A steamer leaves tomorrow. Oh, everything is such a mess."

"Cheer up," Nancy advised. "Six months from now I'm sure you'll be glad you acted as you are doing."

"Miss Drew, you've been a wonderful help to me," young Washburn thanked the girl as he was leaving. "Your advice to me on this trip has been invaluable."

Nancy was glad when the door closed, for she

was blushing furiously at such praise. She was relieved when Bess and George accosted her. The cousins could scarcely wait to question their chum about the snapshot which she had taken of Harold Sand.

"What were you starting to tell us about it just as Mr. Washburn arrived?" Bess asked, studying the picture once more.

"Did I say anything?" inquired Nancy innocently.

"You intimated there was something peculiar about the man's pose. You mentioned his hands."

"Oh, so I did." Nancy laughed in a teasing way. "Don't you notice anything?"

"Not a thing."

"Neither do I," contributed George. "What is so significant about this snapshot, Nancy?"

"Unless I'm very much mistaken it will be the means of solving Mr. Sand's identity."

"His identity!" gasped Bess. "Do you mean to tell me Mr. Sand isn't Mr. Sand?"

"I think it's time you clear up all this mystery," George added irritably. "Why keep us in the dark?"

"I'll do it the next time we see him," Nancy promised with sudden decision. "I agree that this affair has gone far enough."

"Let's find Mr. Sand now," proposed Bess, pulling the other two girls toward the door.

They went to the young man's bedroom and

knocked, but there was no response. They searched along the river and in the garden, but could find no trace of the man anywhere.

"He must have gone into B. A. again," said Nancy. "We'll watch for him when he returns."

Late evening found Harold Sand's bedroom still dark. Nancy and her chums arose early the next morning hoping to meet the man at breakfast. Manuela told them that he had not returned during the night.

"Perhaps he won't come back at all," George said anxiously. "Nancy, tell us what you have discovered."

"I may be wrong, so I'll wait until I see Harold Sand."

"But if we never see him again?"

"We will," said Nancy, smiling confidently.

All morning the girls kept watch for the young man, but in vain. After luncheon Nancy announced she was tired of waiting.

"I am only wasting valuable time," she declared. "The thing I should do is run into the city and visit the luggage shop of Halifax and Lopes."

"We'll go with you," Bess offered quickly.

Nancy shook her head. "The clerks would recall your visit yesterday and be suspicious. Of course, I am known to Mr. Halifax, but I'll try to keep out of his way."

"Don't get into trouble," Bess called anxiously as the girl drove off in a taxi a few minutes later. "We'll worry about you every second until you get back."

Despite the warning of her chums, Nancy had no thought that she would encounter difficulty in learning whether or not her trunk was being held at the luggage shop. She was taken aback when upon dismissing her driver at the door of the shop, she saw a man watching her from the window.

As she hesitated, the Venetian blinds were closed. A curtain dropped over the glass portion of the front door. Several times Nancy tried the door and knocked but could arouse no one.

"I've been recognized by Mr. Halifax," she told herself. "He's afraid if I get inside I may learn too much."

Nancy was more than ever convinced that her missing trunk would be found inside the shop. Pretending to leave, she walked down the street to the corner. Turning, she slipped into an alleyway and came back to the same building.

Upon testing a rear door, Nancy was elated to find it unlocked. Softly she opened it and tiptoed inside.

She found herself in a large storeroom which was cluttered with empty packing boxes. Cautiously she made her way to the customers' room. It too was deserted, but from a private office not far removed she could hear a low murmur of voices.

Nancy was satisfied that her chums had done a thorough job of inspecting the new trunks which were on display, so she did not waste any time looking at them. Instead, she slipped into the repair department. Only three trunks were in the room, and a glance convinced the girl that hers was not among them.

"My hunch was wrong after all," she thought in disappointment. "Now to get out of here before I am discovered."

In her haste to leave the building, Nancy failed to notice a tall pile of heavy leather bags which had been stacked on a shelf above the door. As her shoulder accidentally struck the edge of a table, the resulting vibration caused the bags to teeter.

Before Nancy was even aware of her danger, down fell the luggage. One of the bags struck her squarely on the head. Without making a sound she slumped to the floor.

A long while later when Nancy opened her eyes, the room was dark. She sat up, rubbing her bruised forehead. For a moment she could not remember where she was nor what had happened. Then, as things gradually came back to her, she became aware of voices in the adjoining room.

She could hear two men talking earnestly. With a start she recognized Harry Halifax's voice.

"We must get that girl's trunk if we have to steal it, understand? Your American friend certainly bungled the job from the minute it got on the *Patrician*."

"He did indeed," the other agreed grimly, speaking with an accent. "Si, si, we handle this ourselves."

Was the speaker Senor Lopes?

Nancy heard an outside door open and close. She knew the men had left the shop.

After a moment she pulled herself to her feet. Still feeling dizzy, she gripped the table edge for support.

"Now whose trunk were they talking about?" she asked herself. "Either Treldy's or mine, I'm sure of that. And probably it's hers."

Nancy staggered to the front window of the store and looked out. Harry Halifax and his companion had vanished down the street. It was too late to follow them.

"If I only knew where they are going!" she thought. "They may have bungled their job, but I've bungled mine too!"

The girl was even more deeply chagrined when she tried to open the front door and found it locked from the outside. Windows were fastened and barricaded with an iron grillwork.

Hopefully the girl groped her way to the rear door only to discover that it too had been locked. She was trapped in the building.

"I might shout for help," she told herself, "but if I do the police will be called, and very likely I should end up in jail. Such a mess as I've brought upon myself!"

Nancy located the most comfortable chair in the shop and slumped into it. After a moment she sprang up, for it had occurred to her that she might find interesting papers in Mr. Halifax's desk and also a telephone. However, the door to the private office was locked.

"Everything is against me," she thought, returning to her chair. "But I shouldn't grumble, because it's my own fault I'm here."

For some time she sat in the dark room reflecting upon her unhappy situation. A street clock struck the hour of nine. Back at the Purdy home dinner would be over. Her hostess, as well as Bess and George, must be worrying about her long absence. If only they would come in search of her she might be released!

As the possibility of rescue cheered Nancy, her mind turned to other channels. She began to review all the scattered clues which had come into her possession. Suddenly she recalled a scene long forgotten; an incident which now appeared to have direct bearing upon the present situation. With a cry of delight she sprang from her chair.

"Why didn't I think of that before? Of course that's where my missing trunk is! Now I'll *have* to find a way to get out of here!"

As she groped toward the front door, there was a sound behind her. Suddenly Nancy felt faint and slumped to the floor.

CHAPTER XXII

NANCY'S DISAPPEARANCE

At the Purdy home George and Bess became increasingly alarmed over their chum's prolonged absence. When the dinner hour approached and still she did not come, they were convinced something had happened to her.

"If Nancy had been delayed and nothing else she would have telephoned," reasoned Bess. "She never would allow us to worry this way."

Mrs. Purdy shared the girls' uneasiness. Upon learning the purpose of Nancy's visit to the luggage shop, she insisted upon motoring there at once.

"The place is closed, as I expected," Bess said to the others as they came in sight of the sign above the door. "Nancy can't be here."

"We must notify the police," decided the girls' companion. "I am responsible for Nancy, and if anything should happen to her I never would forgive myself."

Officials were consulted immediately and provided with a description of the missing girl. There was nothing that could be done so Mrs. Purdy, George and Bess returned home to wait and hope.

The night wore on slowly. For Nancy's friends there could be no sleep. Mrs. Purdy made a pot of strong coffee. George walked the floor. Bess spent the time crying and running to the door hopefully whenever a car came down the road.

"It's four o'clock," she said finally, going to a window for the hundredth time. "The sun will be up soon. What will we do if the police can't——"

She stopped talking, for just then a taxi drew up at the house. George and Mrs. Purdy joined Bess at the window.

"It's Nancy!" they cried together.

There was a concerted rush for the door. The next moment Nancy, weary and disheveled, was clasped in loving arms.

"Oh, where have you been all this time?" Bess demanded accusingly. "We've been so terribly worried."

"I managed to get into all that trouble you warned me against. Here I am, though, safe and sound, but terribly tired."

While Nancy bathed, changed her clothes, and ate breakfast, she related how she had happened to be locked in the luggage shop.

"How did you finally get out?" asked George.

"I was just going toward the door when I heard a noise. I thought someone was after me. I must have fainted just then—that blow on my head was probably worse than I thought. I came to about three o'clock, lying on the floor where I'd fallen. Pretty soon I caught sight of the watchman. I scratched on the door like an animal does who is trying to get out. He came to investigate and opened the door.''

"Did he ask you many questions?" inquired Bess.

Nancy chuckled softly. "He didn't see me. When he went into the building to find the animal, I slipped out the door.''

"You must have had a dreadful time until you escaped,'' Mrs. Purdy murmured sympathetically.

After the woman had left, Nancy took her chums outside and gave them further news.

"My evening wasn't very pleasant, I admit. Now that it's over, I'm really glad it all happened.''

"You're glad!" exclaimed Bess incredulously.

"Yes. I didn't find my trunk but I have a good idea where it is.''

"Where?"

"Girls, do you remember that day in the telegraph office when Mr. Joslin sent a cable to someone?"

"Yes," nodded Bess, "only at the time we didn't know who he was. The message had your name in it and the day of your sailing. 'Drew La Plata Saturday.' "

"Then later in New York," Nancy reminded her chums, "I saw Mr. Joslin again. He was sending another message which made use of the words Lopes and Imperio.''

Bess leaned across the table. "Then you believe Nestrelda's stepfather has some connection with Halifax and Lopes.''

"I do.''

"Where does Imperio come in?'' asked George, puzzled. "That clue doesn't fit.''

Nancy went to the telephone desk and picked up the directory. Turning to the I's, she scanned the list of names until she came to the one she sought.

"Here it is. The Hotel Imperio. Now, unless my reasoning is all wrong, we'll find Mr. Lopes and possibly Mr. Halifax living at this address. It came to me suddenly that the men would have my trunk at their hotel. I'm going there at once to find out.''

"Wouldn't it be wiser to notify the police?'' Bess suggested nervously.

"I haven't enough proof to turn the case over to them.''

"At least you must not go alone,'' said George. "Bess and I will tag along and see that you don't get into mischief!''

Shortly after nine o'clock Nancy and her chums reached the hotel and talked with a clerk who spoke English. At mention of Mr. Halifax's name the man shook his head.

"No one here by that name.''

"Dear me, did I say Halifax?'' said Nancy,

correcting herself. "I meant to ask if Mr. Lopes has a room here. They are partners, you know."

"Lopes? Yes, we have a man here by that name. But he is out of the city for a few days."

This news pleased Nancy, but she pretended otherwise.

"Oh, how disappointing! Mr. Lopes is keeping a trunk for me, and I must get into it. I can't possibly wait until he returns."

"What else can you do, Miss?"

"Couldn't you let me into the room?" Nancy pleaded in her most beguiling way. "You must have a master key."

"We do have one, but Mr. Lopes left no orders about a trunk."

"He must have forgotten then—so careless of him. In case you doubt me I can describe the trunk."

"What is it like?"

"It is steamer size, brass bound, and has my initials, N. D., also in brass. Please, as a special favor to me will you see if it is in the room?"

The clerk found Nancy's smile hard to resist.

"I don't remember that any such trunk came into the hotel," he answered, frowning. "This is hardly regular, but I'll look in 369 and see if it is there."

The man took a key from the hook and went upstairs. Ten minutes later he returned with the information that the trunk which Nancy sought was in Mr. Lopes's room.

"It will take me only a moment to get what I need," said Nancy in a wheedling tone. "I'll bring the key back again."

"I have no authority—" the clerk began, but his resistance weakened. "Oh, all right, take it. I hope I won't be blamed."

"I'll explain everything to Mr. Lopes when I see him," said Nancy. "I am sure he will understand."

The man's suite on the third floor was one of the most luxurious in the hotel. Heavy carpets padded the floor of the three rooms; the furniture was expensive and new.

"What a glamorous place!" murmured Bess in awe. She moved across the room to peer into the bathroom, an ultra modern study in glass and colored tile.

Nancy led the way to the bedroom. As she opened the door, her gaze immediately fell upon the brass bound trunk.

"It's mine, all right," she declared triumphantly.

"Let's call the police," suggested George.

Nancy shook her head. "I have other plans," she stated mysteriously.

The trunk had been left unlocked, and the lid lifted readily. At first glance Nancy thought that none of her belongings had been touched, but as she looked carefully, she decided that a number of garments had been repacked.

"Does that red scarf belong to you?" questioned Bess, pointing to an article on the top shelf.

"Yes, I bought it in River Heights just before I packed," responded Nancy.

She reached for the scarf. As she lifted it up, a hard object dropped from it onto the carpet.

"A bracelet!" exclaimed George, stooping to retrieve it. "How careless you are with your jewelry, Nancy."

"That bracelet doesn't belong to me," said Nancy quietly. "I never saw it before in my life."

"Then where did it come from?" gasped Bess. "Could Mr. Lopes have put it in your trunk?"

"He must have."

"How could he have unlocked the trunk?" asked George in bewilderment.

"A skeleton key, no doubt." Nancy took the trinket from Bess and examined it closely. "This looks like a valuable piece of jewelry to me. The red stones may be rubies, and the sparkling ones are diamonds."

"Take it for evidence and let's get out of here," George said uneasily.

"I shouldn't care to have this bracelet in my possession."

"You believe it is stolen?"

"That's my guess, George. I'm leaving it exactly where I found it."

Nancy quickly replaced the piece of jewelry under the scarf and closed the trunk. The girls then left the suite, returning the key to the desk clerk.

"Now what is our next move?" asked Bess as Nancy hailed a passing cab.

"We're going back to Mrs. Purdy's. I want to look at Treldy's trunk once more."

Bess and George could not figure out what Nancy hoped to find. They reminded her that a careful search already had been made.

"We may not have looked closely enough," insisted the Drew girl. "For Treldy's sake I trust everything will be all right."

When they reached the house, the girls learned from Mrs. Purdy that during their absence Mrs. Trenton had telephoned. She had left her address and requested that Nancy call her if convenient.

"Perhaps you should contact her at once," suggested her hostess.

"I will," Nancy promised. "I've wanted to get in touch with her for several days."

Upon phoning Mrs. Trenton at the hotel where she was staying, she inquired casually about Doris. The woman hesitated, then offered the information that her daughter had gone away for a visit with friends.

"I wish you would give her a message when she returns," said Nancy evenly. "Tell her I saw Henry Washburn last night. He has been called back to the United States unexpectedly."

"Called home?" Mrs. Trenton echoed in a half frightened voice. "I wonder why?"

"I don't know all the details. I believe it was some matter relating to his father's estate."

Mrs. Trenton's voice held an unsteady tone as she thanked Nancy for the information. After urging her to come for a visit at the earliest possible moment, she hung up the receiver.

"Mrs. Trenton was deeply disturbed to hear that Henry had started for America," Nancy reported to her chums. "Evidently he didn't tell Doris he was leaving."

Closeting themselves in their bedroom, the girls once more examined Nestrelda's trunk, hoping to find some clue that had been overlooked previously. The search was as fruitless as the first one had been.

"What are you looking for, Nancy?" questioned George. "Do you think Treldy might have hidden some jewelry in her trunk too?"

Nancy did not reply, for at that moment there came a light tap on the door. Before she could open it the maid peered in.

"He's here now," Manuela whispered.

"Who is here?" inquired Nancy patiently.

"Senor Sand. You have been asking for him every day."

"So I have," agreed Nancy, laughing. "Well, thank you for telling me."

"You'll find him in his room," the maid added as she slipped out the door.

"What would we be doing with Mr. Harold

Sand?" chuckled Bess when they were alone again. "He's just another mystery."

Nancy closed down Nestrelda's trunk and arose to her feet.

"You're wrong this time, Bess," she said dramatically. "Follow me, and I'll prove the truth of my words!"

CHAPTER XXIII

NIGHT PROWLERS

LEADING the way to the bedroom across the patio, Nancy knocked boldly on the door. There was no response from within.

"He must be here," whispered Bess.

Nancy determined upon a ruse. Disguising her voice and trying to speak as if she were the maid, she called:

"Senor Sand! Senor Purdy would like to see you."

The door opened almost at once. Before the astonished Mr. Sand could protest, the Drew girl marched into his room.

"Good morning, Miss Trenton," Nancy greeted, calmly seating herself in the nearest chair.

Bess and George stared at their chum in astonishment, wondering if she had lost her mind.

"You seem to have made a mistake," began the young man.

Nancy cut him short. "It's useless, Doris. I've known your identity a long time. Please remove your wig."

The two gazed steadily at each other; then Harold Sand's eyes fell.

"You win, Nancy. I might have known I couldn't fool you."

Bess and George were dumbfounded at the sudden change of voice, and were even more bewildered when Miss Trenton stripped a man's wig from her head.

"I'll have to find another way of hiding from Henry Washburn," she said dolefully. "It was such a jolly little game."

"Sorry to have spoiled your fun," replied Nancy, "but from now on you'll not need to hide from Henry. He has returned to the States."

"He left without letting me know!" Doris cried, her voice revealing both relief and annoyance. "Why didn't he tell me he was going?"

"Perhaps he's found a new love," Nancy suggested mischievously. "How would you feel about that?"

"I—hardly know," Miss Trenton said slowly. "Father always insisted that I marry Henry. Perhaps that was the reason I felt so reluctant."

"Why in the world did you come here in your disguise?" questioned Bess, who felt nothing had been explained.

"It was as good a place to hide as any other. Mrs. Purdy was my governess years ago, so I took her into the secret. I thought my disguise a very clever one."

"It was," said Nancy, smiling.

"Then how did you guess my secret?"

"The camera revealed it. I took a snapshot of you one day when you weren't aware I was near. You sat just as you do now, with your hands folded on your lap."

"A habit of mine," laughed Doris. "I never dreamed that would betray me. I felt quite sure of myself after you failed to penetrate my disguise on other occasions."

"We thought you were the person you were going to elope with!" blurted out Bess.

Nancy tried to cover this remark with a laugh, but it was no use. Deciding it would be better to tell the young woman what she knew, she related her so-called "commission" to try to keep Doris from a hasty marriage with some one other than Henry Washburn.

"I don't know where anyone got an idea I planned to elope," laughed the former Harold Sand.

When Nancy spoke of Mrs. Trenton's telephone call, Doris sprang to her feet and began changing into feminine attire.

"I must go to her at once," she declared anxiously. "Mother will be greatly disturbed to learn that Henry has returned to America."

When Doris urged the girls to accompany her to the hotel they were glad to comply with the request, hoping they might gather additional information. They found Mrs. Trenton in tears. Nothing her daughter could say seemed to comfort her mother.

"No, no, there isn't a thing you can do to clear

up this dreadful situation,'' wailed the distressed woman. ''The entire story will come out and our name will be dishonored!''

''Mother, consider what you are saying——''

''I can't go on this way another day, Doris. Everyone will soon know that the affairs of Trenton and Washburn have been in a bad state for over a year. The business had begun falling off even before Henry's father died.''

''Mother, it isn't as bad as you think! Please——''

''No, don't try to quiet me, Doris. I have thought about this matter a long while. Now that Henry has been called back he will find out the truth. The entire story must come to light.''

''Mrs. Trenton, how did you learn that your husband's firm was in financial difficulty?'' Nancy inquired quickly. ''He told you himself?''

''Oh, no, Doris discovered it. She is very clever with figures, not at all like myself. She examined my husband's books and looked through his stock of luggage.''

''I learned that Father had tried to recoup some serious losses by selling inferior goods at standard prices,'' Doris revealed reluctantly. ''He had branched out into foreign trade. What troubled me was that he seemed to be involved with questionable firms, and that Henry had become a pawn in his hands.''

''Doris made up her mind to do a little detective work,'' Mrs. Trenton resumed. ''Naturally she feared my husband would guess what she was about. She adopted a disguise whenever she had special work to do."

"Were you trying it out that day in River Heights when your car struck mine?" asked Nancy.

"Yes. I was getting Harold a passport. I was frightened lest you might guess that I was a girl. It worried me when you followed me to my hotel in New York."

"I wanted to return the fifty dollars," said Nancy, "and ask you some questions."

"You are welcome to the money, Nancy. I have put you to so much trouble that I am sure you have earned it twice over. I never cared about the fifty dollars. I was more worried that you would discover the identity of your red-haired friend."

"Yet you came to Mrs. Purdy's home where I was staying."

"I had no idea you would be there. After I had made all arrangements with Mrs. Purdy it was too late for me to change my plans. I avoided you as much as I could."

"Doris has learned a great deal here in Buenos Aires," Mrs. Trenton went on. "She visited several luggage firms, and by pretending to represent ours she gathered alarming data. In one place the owner actually looked frightened when she mentioned my husband's name."

"Halifax and Lopes?" asked Nancy.

"Yes. How did you guess it?"

"I've learned rather disturbing facts about them myself," Nancy returned evasively. "Tell me, did Mr. Trenton ever have business dealings with a man named Joslin?"

"I'm not so sure," answered Mrs. Trenton.

"He did, Mother," broke in Doris. "I have seen Mr. Joslin's name on Father's account book."

"Who is he?" questioned Mrs. Trenton anxiously. "Has he a bad reputation?"

"It is not of the best, I fear," said Nancy seriously.

"Oh, dear, then my husband must be in deeper trouble than we thought him to be. When Henry learns the truth he may try to have him arrested." Mrs. Trenton dabbed at her eyes with a handkerchief.

"Father never meant to be dishonest, I know," said Doris earnestly. "But if the story should appear in the newspapers, our reputation will suffer."

"Other innocent persons will suffer too," answered Nancy. "Treldy, for instance. She seems to have no idea that her stepfather may be mixed up in dishonest dealings."

"And poor Mrs. Purdy," added Bess sadly. "She and Mrs. Joslin are half sisters."

"For that matter," contributed George, "Senora Zola is related to the Joslins too. What a dreadful story if it all should come out!"

"What has Mr. Joslin done?" Mrs. Trenton asked between sobs.

"I can't tell you now." Nancy turned toward the door, motioning for her chums to come with her. "But I will promise this—I'll do anything I can to keep the story from getting in the papers."

"You are very kind," Doris murmured gratefully. "I know we can trust you."

"I'll try in every way to keep the Trenton name from being disgraced. But don't tell anyone what you have learned about your father's affairs."

With such valuable information in her possession Nancy knew exactly what she would have to do. Accompanied by Bess and George, she went to a telephone office and made a call to her father in River Heights. She told him of the latest developments in the case, pleading with him to interview Mr. Trenton and urge the man to take such action as would save his family name before it should be too late.

"But Nancy," protested Mr. Drew, "I can't make such a demand without evidence. I have learned a number of things, though hardly enough to warrant such interference on my part."

"Dad, I have evidence, and I soon hope to obtain more. I'm almost certain Mr. Joslin is involved in the smuggling of jewels. We both know he is dishonest."

"I'll talk with Mr. Trenton and do what I

can," Carson Drew promised with sudden decision. "I only hope your evidence will stand up, Nancy."

The telephone call being completed, the three girls returned to Mrs. Purdy's home. Bess and George could not understand why their chum refused to notify the police.

"At least you could tell them about the diamond bracelet in your trunk," argued Bess. "Then they would arrest Mr. Lopes."

"He might claim the bracelet belonged to me since it was found in my trunk. No, I have another plan."

She completely mystified her friends by moving Nestrelda's brass bound trunk into an empty bedroom adjoining her own. She left the door open and did not lock the windows.

"You're inviting a robbery," declared Bess in protest.

"Perhaps I am. Let's wait and see."

Nancy was glad that with Treldy leaving the city there would be no occasion to involve the girl in her stepfather's affairs. Sooner or later she would have to be told the truth, but at least her holiday would not be spoiled.

That entire evening Nancy was very tense. She tried to read but could not. At ten o'clock when members of the household were ready to retire she offered to lock up the place for the night.

Deliberately the girl left a rear door unfastened, then went to her room. Long after everyone else was asleep, she lay awake staring at a patch of moonlight which flooded the floor. She dared not let herself fall into a slumber. If she should doze off even for a few minutes all her plans might go awry.

The hours wore on slowly. In the hall Nancy heard a clock strike two. Presently she became aware of another sound—stealthy footsteps on the patio.

The girl remained still as the door of her room opened a tiny crack. A long moment of waiting, and it swung wider. Two shadowy figures glided across the floor, pausing not six feet from the bed. A flashlight played momentarily over Nancy's face. Then the two men moved through the open doorway to the empty bedroom.

CHAPTER XXIV

HELP FROM CARSON DREW

NANCY slid from her bed. Awakening her chums, she warned them in a whisper to remain quiet.

"Two men are trying to steal Treldy's trunk! We must capture them!"

The three girls tiptoed to the doorway of the empty room. As the intruders came out carrying the heavy piece of luggage between them, Nancy gave the signal. With one accord the chums hurled themselves upon the men.

"Help! Help!" screamed Bess as she was flung roughly aside. "Burglars!"

The girls had not thought the men were so strong. Bess and George were sent sprawling on the floor, but Nancy clung to her quarry. She was dragged several feet before her grip loosened. Then to her chagrin both men bolted. Scrambling from the floor, the girls ran after them, but no one was in sight when they reached the front door.

"Well, we've saved Treldy's trunk at least," Bess gasped, nursing a bruised arm.

"I wanted to catch those men!" Nancy cried. "Oh, I've made a mess of this!"

The entire household had been aroused by the commotion. Lights went on. Manuela could be heard screaming shrilly. In a moment Mrs. Purdy appeared, a robe wrapped about her frail figure.

Nancy was compelled to explain to her what had happened. She did not try to shield herself, but took all the blame for not having locked the doors.

"I did it on purpose," she admitted regretfully. "I thought those men would come here tonight and I wanted to capture them."

"Your plan was a very rash one, Nancy," chided Mrs. Purdy. "You should have called the police. That is what we must do now."

"I suppose so," admitted the girl disconsolately.

Mrs. Purdy telephoned headquarters, receiving a promise that detectives would be sent out early in the morning.

"I almost wish those thieves had taken the trunk in the first place," the woman declared to Nancy. "Since it was brought into this house we've had no peace."

Nancy felt very downhearted, realizing that she had disturbed the tranquility of the household, and to no purpose. She had not even been able to establish the identity of the two intruders, although she had a feeling that the men were connected with the luggage firm of Halifax and Lopes.

"Dad was expecting me to gain definite evidence," she told her chums. "What will he say when he learns I let the culprits get away?"

"That wasn't your fault," declared George staunchly. "You planned it well, but luck was against you."

While the girls were at breakfast, Nancy was surprised to receive word that her father was calling her from the United States. She went to the telephone, wondering what she should tell him. Her gloom gave way to delight as he rapidly recounted his progress on the case.

"Mr. Joslin was arrested here last night," Carson Drew reported tersely. "I've questioned him and he has admitted carrying on smuggling activities."

"Did he implicate Mr. Trenton, or the firm of Halifax and Lopes?" Nancy queried eagerly.

"No, Joslin refuses to name any person associated with him. I want you to notify the authorities and work on the case from that end."

"The police are coming here this morning."

"Good! Tell them the entire story and demand the arrest of Halifax and Lopes."

"I'll do it," promised Nancy instantly.

Before she could mention to him what had occurred during the night, Carson Drew had said good-bye and terminated the connection. Anxiously Nancy awaited the arrival of the police. Shortly after nine o'clock two detectives drove up in an official car. They inspected Nestrelda's trunk, talked with Mrs. Purdy, made a routine inspection of the bedroom which had been entered, and listened attentively to Nancy's story. They seemed so impressed that it came as a shock to her when one of the officers who could speak English said:

"This is all very interesting, but where is your proof, Senorita?"

"My proof?" Nancy was taken aback. "Why, I've just told you all I know."

The policeman shook his head, smiling in an amused way.

"In Argentina a man is considered innocent until he is proven guilty. We cannot arrest a person just because you request it. The firm of Halifax and Lopes is an old, reliable one."

"The men have traded on the firm's reputation!" Nancy protested with spirit. "Actually they are smugglers of jewels!"

"We cannot arrest them without any proof."

"I can show you a bracelet I am certain was stolen," Nancy said in desperation. "Would that be sufficient proof?"

"It might be," the policeman replied cautiously. "Where is the bracelet?"

"In a trunk at the Hotel Imperio."

Bess and George feared that Nancy might involve herself in some trouble by revealing that the stolen bracelet had been hidden in her own luggage. As it developed, their fears were well founded. Upon taking the girls to the Hotel Imperio the detectives inspected the brass bound trunk from top to bottom. They took note of the initials N. D., as well as the tag bearing Nancy's name.

"This is my trunk," she acknowledged frankly, "but it was stolen from me."

"What about the bracelet?"

"It must have been hidden in the trunk by a representative of the firm of Halifax and Lopes."

The detectives already had learned from hotel officials that the suite was rented in the name of Mr. Lopes. Since Nancy's visit there the man had not been back.

"Is that bracelet a stolen one?" inquired Bess as she saw the detectives inspecting it closely. "You must have a list of stolen jewelry."

"It may be," was the cautious reply. "This piece answers a description we have in our possession."

"It seems to me, then, that your duty is perfectly clear," said Nancy impatiently. "Those men ought to be arrested without delay."

"We cannot be certain of your story, Miss Drew. After all, the bracelet was found in your trunk. We know nothing about you save the fact that you are an American tourist."

"It's ridiculous even to hint that Nancy would steal any jewelry!" cried George angrily.

"Would she be likely to bring you here if she had anything to do with the smuggling?" added George.

Nancy did not allow her emotions to overpower her. "It will be very easy to check up on me," she said in a quiet voice. "I live in a place called River Heights where my father is a lawyer. Any number of persons there will vouch for my honesty."

"And for her ability as a detective too!" interposed Bess. "Why, Nancy has solved no end of mystery cases. She could clear this one up if you'd give her a chance."

The policemen were more than half convinced, yet they maintained a conservative attitude toward the affair. Though they seemed satisfied that Nancy had acted in good faith, they were reluctant somehow to make out warrants for the arrest of Halifax and Lopes.

"The firm is a very reliable one," one of them kept repeating. "We must move carefully."

"While you are doing that, the guilty persons will be moving swiftly," retorted Nancy, finally losing her patience. "Even now those men may be trying to get out of the country."

"We cannot act without more convincing evidence."

Nancy was almost in despair, for she had told the detectives everything she knew about the case. She had nothing additional to offer them.

"We may as well go," said George gloomily.

"Wait!"

Nancy turned again to the policemen. "If you were to find an entire cache of stolen jew-

els, would you believe my story?" she asked
excitedly.

"Can you produce the jewels?"

"I think I can," said the girl mysteriously.

"Where are they hidden?"

"In the trunk those men attempted to steal
last night."

"But we searched it ourselves and found
nothing there," objected Bess.

Nancy smiled triumphantly. "I have a new
idea," she declared. "Follow me, and I'll show
you where the jewels are secreted."

CHAPTER XXV

The Secret of the Trunk

Bess and George were more than a little disturbed by Nancy's claim that she could produce the smuggled jewelry. They knew she had made several attempts to locate a false bottom in the trunk, but had failed to do so. How, then, could she hope to produce the stolen articles at a moment's notice?

Nancy displayed no uneasiness as the party motored to the Purdy home. Arriving there, she confidently went to the kitchen and asked for a hammer and a chisel.

"What are you going to do?" Bess whispered in her ear. "Can you really produce the jewelry?"

"If my hunch is correct, I can."

Nancy led the way to Nestrelda's trunk. While the others watched she began prying off the brass trimmings.

"Here, let me do that," offered one of the detectives, quickly catching her idea.

Taking the tools from Nancy, he pried away a narrow strip of brass binding.

"Nothing here," was his brief comment.

214

"Try these initials—N. D.," suggested Nancy hopefully.

The detective pried loose one of the letters. Several small round objects tumbled to the floor and rolled into a corner.

"Pearls!" cried Bess, running to pick them up.

"Perfectly matched!" added the detective, taking them from her. "They've been removed from a necklace."

The men then went to work with a will. Soon every inch of the brass trimming had been removed from Nestrelda's trunk. Concealed beneath it they found diamond rings, unmounted gems, a second necklace, and a bracelet which the girls instantly recognized as familiar to them.

"It's the one stolen from the New York jewelry store!" cried Bess triumphantly. "I guess that proves the Joslins are responsible for this thievery."

"Are you satisfied?" Nancy quietly asked the detectives. "Now will you arrest Mr. Halifax?"

"Si, Senorita. He and Lopes will be picked up at once. Are you certain you can prove they worked hand in hand with Joslin?"

"My father will forward all the proof you need," Nancy replied. "The important thing is to catch those men before they flee the country."

With Buenos Aires police at work on the case,

the three girls considered their responsibility to be at an end. Before nightfall Mr. Halifax and his partner were taken into custody. As was expected, both men protested their innocence, though sufficient evidence had been produced to hold them prisoners.

Mr. Drew remained in close touch with the Argentine authorities by means of telephone and cable. Within a few days he was able to forward documentary proof definitely establishing the guilt of the men and their connection with Mr. Joslin.

In an air mail letter to Nancy the lawyer gave a detailed account of everything that had happened in River Heights during her absence. Nestrelda's stepfather had signed a confession admitting his part in the jewel smuggling, implicating both Lopes and Halifax. He acknowledged being the master mind of an international group which had sought to defraud many firms and individuals. Jewels had been stolen or acquired at low prices and either re-sold at great profit or smuggled into foreign countries.

Nancy was not surprised to learn that Joslin had made contact with luggage firms he knew to be facing financial difficulties. By one means or another he involved them in unscrupulous schemes. When they had been deeply mired he resorted to blackmail, threatening them with exposure unless they complied with his orders.

"Was that what happened to the Trenton and Washburn firm?" Bess inquired of Nancy.

"Yes, Joslin first gave Mr. Trenton a large order for the manufacture of brass bound trunks. Each piece of luggage was so built that it could be used for smuggling jewelry. As I understand it, Mr. Joslin has never paid for the work."

"It is in Mr. Trenton's favor that he never accepted any money. Isn't it strange that he failed to suspect how deeply he might be implicated?" remarked George.

"He must have realized the risk he was taking," said Nancy. "That was why he tried to keep Henry Washburn entirely in the dark about the business. I imagine Mr. Trenton was so worried about finances that he couldn't resist picking up a fat order whenever one would come his way."

"What will happen to him now? Will he be arrested for assisting Joslin in his dishonest schemes?"

"Dad hopes to clear the Trenton name. Fortunately, Mr. Trenton made only one trunk in the order."

"And that one was Nestrelda's?"

"Yes, it was a copy of my own, which I am convinced is a genuine piece of work. I've examined the brass trimmings and find them to be solid. Mr. Joslin planned to try out the special trunk and see how successful it was before having any others manufactured."

"He made his mistake in permitting the luggage to be marked with your initials."

"That was accidental, of course," smiled Nancy. "If Nestrelda had used her step-father's name, I might never have entered the case."

"What will happen to Treldy and her mother?" inquired Bess soberly.

"Mrs. Joslin will escape a sentence. She only followed her husband's orders. The first one of those was to keep me from going on the trip! Also, he forced her to try to steal jewelry, but she was never successful."

Bess, who had been listening without comment to the explanation, now spoke of Henry Washburn and the embarrassing situation at the moment confronting him.

"Marriage with Treldy is out of the question," declared Nancy. "He should be glad he left here without proposing to her."

"He has you to thank for saving him from that," said George. "Treldy wasn't his type, and he doubtless realizes it now."

"I can't believe that Treldy really loves Henry," added Nancy reflectively. "She is too young in her ideas to be sure of her own feelings."

Several weeks later it became known that, due to the young man's cooperation with Carson Drew, the firm of Trenton and Washburn would be saved from humiliation. All his difficulties being straightened out, Henry planned to take a more active part in managing the business.

His new attitude was especially pleasing to Doris, who finally agreed to marry him.

Nancy and her chums were deeply concerned over Treldy's future. They felt very sorry for her, knowing how deeply shocked she would be by the dishonesty of her parents. Nancy had a long talk with Mrs. Purdy, who shared her viewpoint that it would not do for the girl to return to the United States for some time. She must not learn the ugly story.

"I will stay in Buenos Aires until the case has been forgotten," the kindly woman announced. "Treldy needs discipline and I shall provide it, together with loving care."

"Will you have enough money to carry out your plans?" asked Nancy.

"Treldy has a small income of her own left her by her father, Mr. Darlington. That will be sufficient to send her to a school in South America. I know just the place for her."

With Nestrelda's problem solved, Nancy and her chums agreed that their worries were pretty much at an end. Gaily they made plans for a delightful holiday, and unpacked the brass bound trunk which police had brought over from the Hotel Imperio.

"How nice it is to have my own clothes again," laughed Nancy. "If this trunk had been missing much longer I couldn't have worn my dresses, they would have been so out of date!"

Her chums were delighted to see their friend so lighthearted again. Personally they hoped she would not involve herself in a mystery very soon, but Nancy was not the type to stay away from one. Her arrival in River Heights was to herald "The Mystery of the Moss Covered Mansion."

"We'll have a wonderful time now and really see South America," declared George, who was helping her chum to hang up her garments. "But I would feel a lot better if you would get rid of this old thing."

"Old *thing?*" Nancy pretended to glare at her friend. "Are you referring to this lovely piece of luggage?"

"Why don't you sell it and buy a new trunk?" suggested Bess mischievously. "One which can't possibly get you into further trouble."

"Oh, she never would like that sort of a trunk," said George.

"Indeed I shouldn't." Nancy smiled as she lowered the lid. "Anyway, Hannah prophesied I should bring it home packed with mysteries! I can't disappoint her, you know."

THE END